Kindling does
for firewood

Penelope Aitkin

Richard King was born in 1968 and lives in Melbourne. His play *The Life and Death of Yorick the Fool* was performed at the 1994 Adelaide Fringe Festival. *Kindling does for firewood* is his first novel.

Kindling does for firewood

Richard King

ALLEN & UNWIN

To my parents, Helen and Leo.

Publication of this title was assisted by The Australia Council,
the Federal Government's arts funding and advisory body.

First published in 1996 by
Allen & Unwin Pty Ltd
9 Atchison Street, St Leonards, NSW 2065 Australia
Phone: (61 2) 9901 4088
Fax: (61 2) 9906 2218
E-mail: 100252.103@compuserve.com

National Library of Australia
Cataloguing-in-Publication entry:

King, Richard, 1968–
   Kindling does for firewood.

   ISBN 1 86448 168 4.

   I. Title.

A823.3

Set in 11/13 pt Palatino by DOCUPRO, Sydney
Printed by Australian Print Group, Maryborough, Victoria

10 9 8 7 6 5 4 3 2 1

Acknowledgements

I would like to thank all my friends and family for their support and encouragement over the years and, in particular, Janiece and Michael Hardy, Jessie Wakefield, Irene King, Shane Lucas, and Peter and Jennifer Caldwell.

I would also like to acknowledge the considerable debt this novel owes to Mr J. M. Barrie and his story *Peter Pan and Wendy* from which I quote and from which I have drawn many character names, puns, anagrams, similes and situations. With great thanks then, to Mr Barrie.

I

'This ought not to be written in ink
but in a golden splash.'

Peter Pan
J.M. Barrie

When my cousins and my sister and I played our games together on Christmas Day and on our family birthdays, the best person to be if you were a boy was Peter Pan. Captain Hook was fun as well (actually Captain Hook was pretty grouse, the accent is an actor's dream) and to be a Lost Boy was kind of okay. Our dog Bert always seemed to enjoy being the crocodile with the ticking clock, but Peter Pan was best. You were in every scene, you were the centre of the action, and you got to wear a green plastic garbage bag.

And when my cousins and my sister and I gathered and played together on Christmas Days and on birthdays, the best person to be if you were a girl was Aunt Peggy.

Aunt Peggy was my Grandmother's oldest sister and she died when my Grandmother was nine years old.

(Great) Aunt Peggy was beautiful. She was a princess. She was an angel.
    And she always died. She died with a rose clutched to her breast. She died in a rocket explosion. She died surrounded by Indians and kidnapped by cannibals and in earthquakes and tornadoes and tidal waves and tied to the noses of submerging submarines. She once died crossing a desert as my cousin Anthony and I rode past on our bicycles hitting her with long orange plastic pieces of racetrack from my Hot Wheels race course.

That was my Great Aunt Peggy. Who died before I or my mother or my father were born. Who lived forever as a willowed young woman in a sepia photograph on my Grandmother's bookshelf. Trapped and immortal; a glorious and glorified amaranth at the perpetual age of eighteen.

She is the standard, or the absence, by which we and our struggles are judged.

> *She was very beautiful.*
> *She was very young.*
> *She spied against the Nazis.*
> *She fought against pirates.*
> *She was savaged by sharks and strangled by giant squid and suffocated by great clams.*
> *She went down in a plane crash and ate all the other passengers (which was almost greedy on her part as we had her rescued within two days).*
> *She was shot at the Alamo and scorched in the Hindenburg.*
> *She committed suicide when she heard that her lover had died in a duel (that was my sister's idea).*
> *She was eaten by dinosaurs.*
> *And for a time there in the late 1970s she was Darth Vader's sister.*

I wish I had have known her.
I wish I had have had her like me.

Aunt Peggy and my Grandmother and all her family grew up in the North East of Tasmania, the second largest of the many islands that form the nation state of Australia. Tasmania was originally inhabited by savages ('They carry tomahawks and knives, and their naked bodies gleam with paint and oil'), but was rediscovered by the British, who saw the 'unclaimed' land and sought a use and found it, and they dispatched the lesser of their infantry and force ('A more villainous-looking lot never hung in a row on Execution dock') to establish and administer a penal colony for a mass of surplus and sundry convicts ('They are the children who fell out of perambulators when the nurse is looking the other way').

The colony became a community, and the community became a society, and the society had one wordless man who sired six children and who tried to farm a land where the trees were as hard as stone, and the ground was harder than the trees, and the hens lay stale eggs that sunk like a rock in a pot of water. His eldest daughter dreamed of birds that made their nests in men's broadbrimmed hats, of jealous faeries, and mermaids who sang on rocks and who slept in coral bedchambers with doors that rang a tiny bell whenever they opened or closed.

His eldest daughter pushes my Grandmother in her pram down the Big Hill and the pram stumbles over and 'crash' and my Grandmother falls into the muddy ditch. His oldest daughter pulls restlessly at the teats of the old and thin calimanco cow and wearily tosses the mucksen washing water down the gully-trap and listens with dreaming-eyes to the tall-tales and yarns of the itinerant cadators who with some regularity pass by the small lustreless farm.

And his eldest daughter always dies.

The proof of her glory and the proof of her magic was manifested in the grand and splendid life lived by my Aunt Boo, who was Peggy's daughter. Aunt Boo lived in a great white mansion with grand and expansive gardens: broad, green trees and healthy, but slightly uptight and distracted, rosebushes, and colourful, bright flowerbeds.

One day when visiting my Aunt Boo I plucked another flower and ran with it to my mother.

She put her hand to her heart and exclaimed, 'Oh you darling boy. Why can't you remain like this forever!'

I showed it to my sister.

'Those flowers talk to each other, you know,' my sister said, and I believed her because she was older.

'What do they talk about?'

'They talk about how much they all hate you.'

5

When my mother took my Grandmother and my sister Julia and myself to visit Aunt Boo we would walk through her gardens and talk to the people in their nightwear. Our cousins would never believe us when we told them of Aunt Boo's mansion where she lived in her pyjamas, and of the nuns who would go and fetch her when we came, and who would take her back to her bedroom.

And then we'd play games where we were Aunt Boo's servants, and my cousin Sandra would be the head nun, because she was overweight and always got the character parts (she was a very good bo'sun Smee by way of example). And then we'd sit and mix poe-poe juice and mammee-apple cordial with water and pretend we were a chemist shop.

That's what I remember.

William

At the beginning of this story I'm standing in a small and
cluttered, charming and fusty bookshop, idling away a few
moments flicking through a copy of *Where's Wally Now?*
when an attractive woman who looks in her mid-twenties,
with brown hair and milky coffee-coloured freckles that
splay across and over her nose and cheeks and down and
onto her neck and cleavage, walks up to me and says:

— Excuse me. Can I ask, have you read this book?

She is holding up a copy of Jung Chang's *Wild Swans*.
I answer:

— Yes.

— Is it as good as it's cracked up to be?

— No.

— No?

— Shit no.

— Oh, she responds and pauses for a moment, slightly
bushwhacked by the surprising zealousness of my reply
in the negative. I add:

— It's all right, I suppose. It's a good yarn. I guess it's
a great yarn. But I don't know . . . it's sort of . . . ish.

— Ish?

— Ish-ish. I haven't read it actually.

— Why did you lie about having read it?

— For fun.

— And was lying to me about having read it fun?

— No. Not really. Not at all.

She stands and looks at the cover of the book, giving
attention to the photographs of the grandmother, mother
and daughter, whose individual and contrasting lives the

book chronicles, and which are arranged vertically on the cover, looking considerably like some faction of an Oriental 'Brady Bunch' clan. The green cover and portraits obviously reveal nothing to refute or affirm my uninformed review, and the pretty girl with the light freckles that dust her face and neck and generous cleavage (her skin looking a bit like the celluloid negative of a photograph of a lamington made in a factory where they are slightly miserly when they sprinkle on the desiccated coconut) turns to me and looks up and asks:

— What is good at the moment?

— I don't know.

— Well . . .

— Well I really don't know. What have you read and enjoyed?

— Milan Kundera, Gabriel Garcia Marquez, Marguerite Duras.

I lead the girl with the freckles along the fiction shelves that run one side and up to the rear of the store, and reach down to the bottom shelf and grab a copy of *John Dollar* by Marianne Wiggins.

— Read the back, I say and she takes the book and rests it against her small, taut, perfect, slight paunch that is pressing against her tan blouse. I stand and with my foot trace the outline of a draughthorse that is worked into the carpet and watch her eyes as they skit back-towards and fore-wards over the words like a dragonfly darting over a still pond (Not really. Not much like a dragonfly at all. They looked more like a couple of eyes that were scan-reading something. I think I was trying a bit too hard there.), reading the description of the book on the back cover. I interrupt:

— How's your course going?

She pauses, having registered my interruption, and then makes sense of it:

— Um . . . yeah . . . good. What . . . what course?

— Arts at Melbourne University.

— How did you know I was doing arts at Melbourne?

— Marguerite Duras. Every female arts student at Melbourne University reads Marguerite Duras.

— Oh. Um . . . good. This sounds like *Lord of the Flies*.

— It is. The author read *Lord of the Flies* and thought 'Okay. But that's not how girls would do it. This is how girls would do it.' It's beautiful.

— Really?

— There's one bit where one of the girls is describing a tree, it's got a hive and there's all this honey dripping out of it, and she calls it 'The tree that weeps enjoyments'.

I laugh my black crowing laugh that I'm trying to change, and a few other stray people in the shop look up alarmed and slightly bewildered by the unusual sound and its unlikely source, and then return to their browsing. At the laugh's conclusion there is a brief, uncomfortable moment of silence. I say:

— I can read a whole book just for one phrase like that.

She says:

— You've got a silly laugh.

— I've got a stupid laugh. It's stupid. Luckily I don't laugh very often.

— No?

— I'm good at crying. I've got a great cry.

— Is this any good? she asks, pointing with her foot at a copy of Marina Warner's *The Skating Party* which is also on the bottom shelf.

— No. The jacket is pretty though.

— It's lovely.

— Look, this one's almost the same, I say and pluck out a copy of *In a Dark Wood* to show the girl with the brown hair and the brown freckles and the slightly plump round arse that sits steadily on her thin legs like a calico bag full of walnuts set to rest on an upturned mustard bottle; an upturned mustard bottle that has two long, thin spouts. I say:

— The pretty jackets are done a great disservice by her writing.

— They're that bad?

— No. Not really. They're actually very good. Kind of good. Not as good as Rose Tremain.

— Is that a new *Where's Wally?* she asks, referring to the book I still have in my hand.

— No. It's the second one.

— Fun?

— I think the main character gets a bit lost in the general narrative.

The girl laughs at my joke. I say:

— Your laugh is grouse. It's very pretty. I wish I laughed like that.

— You can borrow it. Okay, I'll take it.

She turns the copy of *John Dollar* sideways and claps her right hand against it. We move over to the small counter and cash register at the front of the shop and I stand behind it and mumble:

— Joh Do, as I press those five letters on the keyboard. She says:

— Joh Do?

— It's a title key. It's the first three letters of the first word, the first two letters of the second word, and then the first letter of any third word. It's how the computer knows what book I'm selling. *John Dollar*. Joh Do.

— Lucky it's not called 'Dillon Dollar.'

I crow my stupid, accursed, shitful guttural laugh and then say:

— We've got a book called *Penelope's Island*.

— Gross. Real gross. Do you give student discount?

10

— Not really. But we've got a People-I-Didn't-Really-Mind-Talking-To discount. It works out at $10.35.

— Thanks.

— I hope you like it. I get a bit oogly-woogly when people buy books I recommend.

— If I hate it I'll come back and change it for a copy of Wil Sw.

— Good. Do.

— Thanks, she says as I press the change into her hand and for just a moment too long rest my fingers on the coins in her palm (a little move from my 'Gentle and Almost Imperceptible Means of Seduction' routine), just enough for her to register and remember this first instant of physical contact between us. When my hand moves away, hers stays suspended in the air for a few seconds.

Margaret

He was good company, and seemed to be a lot like I'd heard him described, but he was far too big for that bookshop. I tested him with the Marina Warners, just plucked them out of the air at random, and it was fairly obvious he'd read them. He is kind of handsome, but not in a way I usually find attractive, with matted curly brown hair and inappropriately small fine eyeglasses. He was wearing a large, sloppy green jumper and brown-green baggy trousers and he smelt of perspiration and soil and play. And quite strongly of marshmallows, which was strange. He didn't recognise me at all although admittedly I'd only met him once. (I'd met him a hundred thousand times.) Andrea hates him, quite correctly, but she hates him with a shy, delighted smile. Elizabeth doesn't like him at all. Says that he can be all serious and conversational and appear to be really interested in what you say, and then all of a sudden he'll hit you with some gross and sleazy move. She said that occasionally it's funny, but more often than not it's just embarrassing.

Says that he's a prick, and a loser, and a fuckwit from hell.

Says that he's pretty much close to the biggest shitsack she has ever met.

Says that the sex is okay.

Just okay.

When we were at the counter we made some more small talk and then it happened. He put the change in my hand and then was almost tonguing-off my palm with his fingers. Gross.

He was looking straight into my eyes, trying to hypno-
tise me I suppose, and I just had to have a go at him so I
said:

— Thank you, William.

— How do you know my name? he asked, he was
pretty surprised. I followed through with the knife:

— William Casey.

— I don't . . . Have we met?

— No . . . well only once. I went to school with Andrea
Stone.

— Oh. Oops.

— It doesn't matter. You seem okay. Despite all the
stories.

— I really need to have a word to my public relations
people hey?

— No. It's okay. People don't really care anymore.

— What's your name?

— Marpa.

— That's unusual.

— It's Hungarian.

— Is it?

— No. It's a title key. Bye William.

— See you Mar Pa, he says, and I leave the store, and
wander straight up to the other bookstore that lies further
up the slight hill, and buy some wrapping paper. I've
already read *John Dollar*, and it is truly a wondrous book,
so I figure it will make a good gift one day.

William

Later that day the telephone rings and I answer it and say;
— Yes. Hello. South End Book Store.
A woman says:
— Hello. I'm after a book. I thought you might have it.
— I can check for you.
— It's called 'Vagmann's Incredible Adventure'.
— We don't have it, I'm sorry.
— Well can you check?
— I know it's not here.
— Well can't you check on the computer and see if you can order it in?
— Okay lady. Just chill.
I type in the title key and give a gruff, half laugh. The woman on the phone says:
— What are you laughing at?
— Nothing. I coughed.
— Oh.
And there's a slight pause at this point and then she continues:
— I thought you might be laughing at the fact that you've just typed the word 'Vagina' onto your computer screen.
— Well I was laughing at that actually. Who is this?
— Mar Pa.
— Margaret?
— That's good. And the Pa?
— Parker?
— Palmer. But you were close. I've started the Marianne Wiggins. It's very good.

14

— Good. Good. I'm glad you like it.

— I'll see you 'round, William.

— Bye, Margaret Palmer.

This story takes place in Melbourne, Australia.

That's where the bookshop is and it's where I live. Yep. Melbourne clutches onto the underside of Australia, and hence, the underside of the world like one of those brown little burs that you get on your socks when you walk through long grass.

Like that?

I guess like that.

A bit like that.

It is the second largest city on the second largest country in the second most important hemisphere of the fifth largest planet of a small solar system of what, we are advised, is a remote and distant galaxy.

We all have a slight chip on our shoulder down here in Melbourne.

It's a nice town with a bit of the grub and stir of a vast city, or maybe a big city that has retained some small community charm.

It has got the buildings of a city; the grand and shiny, mirror-clad skyscrapers of a great and vital metropolis, and yet it has only got the population and incestuous networking of a large rural town.

I can't go into a pub or a nightclub or a TAB without meeting someone who went to school with me, or met me at a party, or played in the same under-14s basketball team as me. (We made it to the semis and then bombed out.)

There's also always the chance that some complete stranger is going to want to punch me up because he's drunk with his mates, hasn't been able to seduce a female, and we've got a Premier who makes everyone angry.

If a woman sits down next to me on a tram and starts conversation, there's a high likelihood she used to work with my father.

If a person runs over my guinea pig, and leaves the poor wretched pancake on my doorstep with a note of apology, it's highly probable that they used to live three streets away from a man I met at university.

And if a pretty girl walks into the bookstore where I work and asks me what I think of a particular book there's always the chance that she went to school with Andrea Stone.

So don't even think about it, William Casey.

Or maybe . . . think about it.

No one ever got in trouble for thinking about a thing.

I am the youngest child of two youngest children.

My father is a remarkably unparticular man, a totally inconsequential fellow of no distinctive quality but for the fact that he has absolutely no memory of what he was doing the moment he first heard that President John F. Kennedy had been shot.

He just cannot remember.

No idea.

And in a world where it is argued that everyone can remember what they were doing when President Jack Kennedy was shot, this memory-hole worries him.

A lot.

He believes that out there in the world there's someone who knows that when they found out that President Kennedy was shot they were with him, at work or in a store or somewhere, and he has tried in vain for the last thirty years to find that person. He believes that when he does find them they will say:

— You remember. We were looking at the watering cans and that little old fellow told us. He had a green cardigan on. Greenish.

And then my dad will say:

— Oh that's right. I'd forgotten. Aren't I a goose.

Or something like that.

My father is a member of a self-help group for other people who likewise have no memory of what they were doing the moment they first heard that President John F. Kennedy had been shot.

They have a newsletter (called 'Lee Harvey Who?') and there is a member who lives in Argentina and one in Norway.

I am my parent's second child. Of two.

I am tall and sweaty and puffily fat.

A bit like a croissant.

I am a Piscean.

And I work in a bookshop.

On the Sunday after the day Margaret Palmer bought a copy of *John Dollar* from the bookshop where I work and then later rang me, I am again working in the bookshop and standing behind the counter where, with little interest or application, I have been ticking off items on a seven-page invoice, when I suddenly, with the sixth sense of the sales assistant, become aware of someone entering the store, and I look up to see Margaret standing at the door, with a smile as huge as the gates to some great fun park. She says:

— Hello, William.

— Hello, Margaret. What are you after today?

— What's good at the moment?

— Not working in a bookshop. Not working in a book-shop would be excellent. Have you read this? I ask

17

Margaret, handing her a copy of Geraldine McCaughrean's *The Maypole*.

— No, I haven't. Pretty cover.

— It is, isn't it.

— Good?

— Absolutely beautiful.

— Okay. How much is it?

— You're easy. Oh. Sorry. I didn't mean that in a sort of 'Benny Hill' sleazy way or anything.

— I didn't take it that way. How much?

— $10.35.

— What do you do when you're not here, William?

— Not where?

— Not here in the shop.

— I'm an astronaut.

— Seriously.

— No. Very light-heartedly. I'm a tongue-in-cheek astronaut.

— What do you really do?

— I don't know . . . watch telly, I guess. I smoke and . . . drink beer and . . .

— Would you like to come and see a play I'm in?

— No way, bitch.

— What?

— I'm being silly. Sure I'd love to. What play is it?

— *Othello*.

— By?

— Some English guy.

— Are you Desdemona?

— No, I'm the prostitute.

— Most fair Bianca.

— Yes.

— 'I' faith sweet love, I was coming to your house.'

— How do you know that?

— I was Cassio in a performance out at Monash a couple of years ago.

— Well that's got a nice sort of . . . touch to it.

(!?!)

She continues:

— It's not much of a part. They've made me the stage manager and costume designer and prompt and everything, I think just to make sure I turn up every night.

— Don't be stupid. Stupid as well as smelly. It's a nice part. A nice cameo.

— Oh well . . . whatever. Anyway I love my aria in it.

— Bianca doesn't sing.

— The director likes my voice so he's given me a song.

— That's a bit strained.

— That's a bit cute actually. Come on the last night and then you can come to the cast party afterwards.

— Um . . . okay . . .

— Next Saturday. It's on at the uni in the Guy Manton rooms at eight o'clock.

— I'll see you then.

— Bye William.

At home that evening I rang up a friend.

— Yes hello.

— Um . . . hi . . . hello. Is Angela available?

— No. It's William isn't it? She's at her classes tonight.

Her classes are French classes. Angela is learning French, for the sole reason that she thinks it would be very elegant to make love in French. Just to be able to cry out or scream or crow in French at the moments of most extreme and greatest passion. When she first told me that this was her only reason for taking a French course I laughed hysterically behind my set and noncommittal face, and then I said with genuine enthusiasm, and in no way letting slip that I thought this the most preposterous and unconscionable strategy I had ever heard: 'Oh. Cool. That's a good idea.'

I have since given it some thought and have myself subsequently decided that, 'Yes, that would be a skill I also would like,' and have sifted through my few multilingual items of hard-core pornography. Not pornography that I carry on my person but rather pornography that has been stored and stashed in a shoe-box at the base of my wardrobe in my parents' home in Blackburn, the legacy of my heady adolescence when my mind and body and every waking moment (and many sleeping ones as testified by the small, stiff stains that marked my pyjama pants when I would wake in the morning), was committed to and obsessed by the remarkable changes and growth and power of my own genitals and sexual persona. A quick study of the pornography (most explicit pornography features photographic sequences/imbroglios/romances that are accompanied by descriptive script in French, English, German and Spanish), and some hasty note-taking, have allowed me to commit to memory the odd phrase or exclamation or outcry, to one day incorporate into my own lovemaking.

— Will I tell her you called?

— No. Um yes. Moira . . . before you go, do we know a girl called Margaret Palmer?

— Yeah, I think she's the one who went out with Bill Jukes.

— Who's Bill Jukes?

— You know. He used to go out with Wendy.

— My Wendy?

— Yes. After you and Wendy broke up she went out with Bill who'd gone out with Margaret. I think Margaret's a bit weird. Nice though. I've only met her a couple of times.

— Oh.

— Why? Have you got a hot date?

— Kind of. Hey Moira, do you know why Angela is taking French?

— She made me promise not to tell anyone, William, but what the heck, it's pretty fucking funny. It's so as she can fuck in French.

— Yeah, I knew already. Moira, is that kind of cool or kind of daggy?

— I'm not sure. I've got her to teach me a few things. Just stuff like 'Oh God, I'm coming, I'm coming' and like 'Fuck this is good! Keep doing that' things. I'm not sure whether I'll ever use them.

— Oh.

— I'll get her to give you a call.

William

This is how the second bit starts. On the Saturday evening I am sitting amidst the tiered seating of the Guy Manton Theatre (a small converted lecture hall whose only claim to theatre status rests on the presence of a few dinky, buzzing stage lights that are attached to the ceiling cross-beams) at Melbourne University, shifting uncomfortably in my seat and stretching my legs having just witnessed the University Shakespeare Society production of *Othello*.

It was woeful. Gloriously woeful.

Woeful with the earnest intent and energy that only a group of simple-minded undergraduates can bring to a production. Most performances of *Othello* tend to be dreadful; it is as if Shakespeare has built into the script a time release poison, a cancer, a destructive mechanism that ensures that any production will have its artistic peak when one participant says 'Why don't we put on *Othello*?' and sees it steadily decline in quality from that point. This particular production, however, tops them all.

It is such an atrocity that it achieves a grandeur. A majesty.

Our Othello is a thin and sinewy pale fellow, tall and ungainly, with long, red hair pulled back in a grimy pony-tail, with small and piggy, eternally squinting eyes, who is blessed, however, with a surprisingly strong and forceful voice which he utilises with a marked ineptitude.

Our Othello does not roar or bellow but rather drones on and on and on.

22

Cassio, whilst a strikingly handsome young man, has a command and presence, off and on the stage, which cries for all witnesses, 'KICK ME'.

Our major protagonists all have large and unwieldy chipboard blocks or trapeziums which they clank around on the stage and then stand upon to deliver their lines.

Iago's is black and Othello's?

White.

See, it's symbolism. Skin dark, heart pure . . . do you get it? Brilliant stuff, you know.

We really have to do something about these undergraduate productions. We can no longer allow Shakespeare to be mongrelised in this manner.

And I suggest we either fill all those persons who are involved in student theatre with a very slow setting cement or we bind them to the fore-end of submerging submarines.

A mention must also be made of another performance in this evening of student theatre: that of the earnest and intense young director, who sat and thoughtfully stroked his piquedevant throughout the performance and who, with paternal appreciation, applauded his cast at its conclusion, and finally, with laudable humility, gracefully accepted that duplicitous applause extended to himself.

Still waters run deep with this fellow.

Prepare to submerge.

Our evening is to a degree salvaged by two details; an Iago who is perhaps five or seven years older than the remainder of the cast, with a head clean of hair, and who brings to his performance a bridled passion and fury that is exhilarating to witness. His performance is weakened in the second half by the sudden and formerly unevidenced presence of a small stain of urine on his tights, a remnant of a far greater quantity which he must have too hastily

23

passed during the interval, and which commands the attention of myself and the rest of the audience as it slowly and gradually dries during the remainder of the play.

Did Desdemona die?

Did Othello fall by his own hand?

I cannot recall with surety. But I can say with certainty that by the curtain call the piss had gone from the nude-noggin's dacks.

And it was an evening enriched by the appearance, and too brief presence, of our Margaret.

She sweeps onto the stage, fires us through her lines, enlivens us to attention, and then too quickly disappears.

Whorish, kind, tender and funny, she was good company.

And correctly, she was rewarded with hearty and genuine applause during her curtain call, applause that to an embarrassing degree revealed the sparse and meagre salutations that greeted her fellow players.

— What did you think? asks Margaret, still wearing her make-up, a display that strides that fine line between rendering her an over-tarted grotesque and that which more discreetly enhances and celebrates her entrancing beauty. She is still wearing her costume, a fine and long black velvet dress with delicate gold trim, and with a plunging neckline and what must be a sturdy bodice that brings her breasts together in a cleavage that is so plump and resplendent that you feel like you want to fry an egg on it.

— I thought it was great (I lie).

— Oh rubbish. It was shocking. Did you see Jason's post-urinal drip during the second act?

— You were good.

24

— Good? I was great actually. I think Emilia and Desdemona hate me. Do you still want to come to the cast party?

— Didn't originally. Don't think I ever did but sure . . . I guess. Thanks. Yes, Margaret.

— Don't say that by the way. Don't ever say my name. It's spooky.

— 'Margaret's not spooky.

— No, not the name itself. It's the . . . 'Oh god I'm being addressed. What, what, what do you want?' thing. It scares me.

— Um . . . cool, but kind of not. Okay.

— Your haircut looks good. You look a lot younger.

— Like only about thirty-five or something?

— No. Accept a compliment when it's given. You look quite handsome.

— Well okay. Thank you.

— I'll just get out of this shit and meet you in a sec.

— Gee, don't. You look wonderful.

— Don't do this flirt shit with me, William. You can if you like. Gentle flirtation at this early stage. I guess that's promising. I'll be back in a moment.*

Margaret went off and got changed and washed the heavy make-up from her face but missed an amount on her neck which was streaky and darker and stained the collar of her white T-shirt which she wore under a houndstooth jacket and which stretched against her rich bust. She was wearing some old blue jeans.

---

* Those were her precise words, so there can be no denying that it was she who first tempted him.

Margaret

We went back to the cast party and both stood around nervous in each other's company. William perhaps uncertain why he'd been invited and why the evening was being wasted in the company of a bunch of undergraduate wankers, and myself uncertain as to why I was so intently trying to bind myself to this particular mast of this particular ship, and what journey I thought I was taking.

When I watch William, and think about what a relationship with him would represent (and I've become pretty certain that's what I'm pursuing here) it's like watching one of those old black and white movies where the young lovers stand on the storm-swept deck of the grand liner, William and I gazing into each other's eyes, our fingers tenderly entwined, and glowing in our dapper clothes with sequins and seams, bands and folds and collars and cuffs glowing in the halo of our mutual adoration, and then walking off to the left or to the right, revealing the life preserver behind us inscribed with the ship's name *Titanic*. A bit like that. Maybe that's stretching it a bit.

This is a bit of the conversation during the early and awkward part of the evening, William leaning up against the wall and clumsily keeping beat with the music, patting one hand against his upper leg and tapping the other foot, me watching as he unknowingly spills great quantities of red wine from the glass he holds in the other hand.

— So, Margaret. What's actually um . . . what's news with you?

— Nothing much.

— Oh . . . okay. Did you go into uni today?

— No.

— Did you work?

— No.

— Why not?

— I wasn't rostered on.

— Oh. When do you work next?

— Monday.

— This Monday?

— Yes.

— Good.

— Not really.

— Oh?

— Yes. It's a bit of a drag really.

— Oh.

— Right.

— What *did* you do today, Margaret?

— Nothing really. Why?

— No reason . . . Just sort of . . . you know . . .

— Oh.

And it is awkward because William and I have got a subtext going. Perhaps we should have kissed by now or fucked by now and then settled into each other's company, not ever really needing to speak to each other again. Or maybe we should never have flirted at all, and thus created a relationship based on a mutual respect and friendship, that could have persevered and endured. (Yadda Yadda Yadda.) That chance of dear friendship has passed. Now we're committed and inescapably bound to this unspoken agenda that underlies any moment's time together, that will smoulder between us until such time as one of us throws caution to the side and stuffs their tongue down the other's gullet like a mother and pelican chick. Or, until one of us just figures, 'I don't need this shit. Look it's been

27

really nice but I've just got to . . . you know . . . I'll give you a call or see you around or something.'

Put your hand on my cheek, William.

Press your lips against mine.

Rest your palm against my breasts.

Do something, you big dweeb.

I compliment him on the wine he has brought to the party.

William

Oh for fuck's sake peanut-brain what are you doing?

Make a pass at this woman, you idiot. Like this is on. It's obviously on.

She hangs around the shop all the time, she's invited you out to this party, like what do you need? A flash of pink and a signed stat dec saying, 'I'm kind of keen on you, Will.' This is embarrassing. She's beautiful. And she's clearly keen. And you've gone all weird and shy. You've done this before. What about . . . what about that girl at the Station Hotel? What was her name? Catherine? No . . . that's not right. Katherine. That's it. Katherine Elizabeth Shanning. So you've done it in the past. Katherine Elizabeth Shanning was just standing there and you didn't even know her and you scored easy. Fuck!! What if Margaret knows Katherine Elizabeth Shanning. Like, sure you scored but you came out of it looking like a bit of an arsehole. Don't worry. You can do this. Just ask her if she wants to stand outside for a while. Or . . . wipe away that broken lash she's got on her cheek. Just establish something. Okay. Okay. This is it. I'll tell you what. You let a five-second silence go, and then if she hasn't talked, you make a move.

28

One . . . two . . .

— This wine's not bad. How much is it? (Fuck Damn.)

— It's usually about thirteen dollars. This was fourteen ninety or something because I had to buy it on the way and it was more expensive there. I usually drink the red label which is about nine dollars but I thought this would be more impressive.

— I am impressed. Most of the guys I go out with bring a thirty dollar bottle of wine to show-off with. This is quite quaint.

— Um . . .

— I was joking, William. I was only shit-stirring. Most of the guys who ask me out have usually drunk a slab of beer before they meet up with me and spend the whole night pissed and horny. Try to be a little bit less uptight.

— I am a bit uptight aren't I?

— Well, there really isn't any need to be. This isn't anything, okay? I just sort of thought you might like to see the play I'm in and I sort of thought you might like to come to the cast party afterwards. It's just fun, okay?

— Shit, Margaret. I'm not fourteen or anything. I knew you weren't proposing or anything. I'm just generally an uptight person.

And I am an uptight person. You know those people who are relaxed and cool about things? I hate them. I can't stand them.

And I have tried relaxing. I've tried relaxing a number of times. I'd get home from work and just get into bed and just relax . . . but then . . . but then my socks would start bothering me. Really annoying me. They're too tight or too scratchy. And then I'd take my socks off and that'd be fine, and I'd stretch and wriggle my toes and then . . . then the fact that my feet didn't have socks on would annoy me. They're so cold and un . . . constricted, and while I was taking my socks off I mussed up the counterpane and now the feathers are all lopsided and while I'm here actually I don't like the frills on the counterpane up this end and I wish those three books on that shelf weren't all black in a row like that and God I wish that dog would stop barking and shit my fridge is noisy and it's too bloody light and . . .

So I figure it's not really worth it trying to relax.

Too much stress.

— Um . . . Margaret. I'm just . . . going to the toilet for a second. Do you want anything or . . . No. Okay. I'll be back in a sec.

You idiot. You're pathetic. Get it together, dweeb. Drink more alcohol. That's the best plan I can think of. Yep. Thing is I've never slept with a girl whose first name finishes with a consonant. Maybe that's why this is so hard.

Margaret

Why did I do that? Why did I go and do that? I think he was almost at the point of trying something and then I shot him down. Why did I do that? This is ridiculous. I don't need this stress. We'll just write this one off. If he was at all interested he would have done something by now so he's obviously not. Like . . . according to Katherine Elizabeth Shanning he hardly beats around the bush when he's got his mind set. Weird that those two slept with each other. So forget it. We'll just have a nice night.

That's okay.

That's cool.

It's fine.

It's a shame.

William

It's gone and it's over. The moment has passed. It was there for a while and we both eagerly and intently stalked it, steadily circling it under the cover of the tall trees as it sat on its haunches in the small clearing and nibbled at the young grass and then . . . I don't know. One of us stepped on a rock that shifted noisily under our weight or cracked a twig, and the moment pricked up its ears and sniffed the air and then raced swiftly down a burrow and out of claiming, its tail pulled in safely between its hind legs, and evading our grasp and pursuit. (Like that? Maybe not. It was a pretty analogy, though.) It's gone and it's over. I returned from the outside toilet, pausing at the window and watching Margaret in the warmth of the room telling stories and tales to the other members of the cast, and then I pushed my way in through the heavy door and sidled up next to her and we both knew the opportunity had passed. It wasn't spoken between us, but it was taken as said, and we then relaxed into each other's company, warmly chucking each other under the chin, relieved at the death of the awkward silence and the hateful telling.

I got drunk. Fuck I got smashed. I got really pissed and stole Desdemona's cloth that she had used to remove her stage make-up after each performance, and which was stuffed in her bag which she had stashed on the first floor landing and then I hid it in the bedroom of the actor who played Cassio, and in whose house we were having this cast party. I then traipsed up the stairs her shy and pimply boyfriend and subtly brought it to his attention. He just laughed and said, 'Oh I see. This is kind of like what happens in the play. Good one, Will.'

31

Well, it was a good one. It was kind of funny. Actually it was very funny. The least he could have done was get really jealous and kill her.

Margaret got as pissed, if not more so, and got in a fight with the director and set fire to his goatee, burning it all off and some.

I vomited out in the backyard for some twenty minutes and Margaret sat patiently, and with some kindness, beside me for the duration, steadily rubbing my back. The compliment was returned about an hour later when she suddenly cut off conversation mid-sentence and wheeled off from the small group in which we stood, raced up the stairs and I sat by her on the edge of the rust-stained bath as she coughed up ample portions of partly-digested food, her eyes teary and bloodied.

After a while we called a taxi.

Margaret

After a while I said 'Can we call a taxi?' and after he had, we sat silently out on a couch on the cold front porch of Cassio's house, William pulling absent-mindedly on stray, torn bits of stuffing that were poking out from the cushions on which we sat, and me fighting forlornly against this fucking huge, mega-pissed thunderstorm that was playing havoc with my head.

William

The taxi ride was conducted largely in silence, both of us ruminating on our own separate and independent interpretations of the evening (not the taxidriver. I have no idea what he was thinking about. Maybe football or telephone and gas bills or maybe mooses), me favouring this or that particular version, and praising the fact that for whatever happened we didn't jeopardise or risk whatever friendship we have.

Her . . . well, I don't know what she was thinking.

Margaret

You are quickly running out of time, fuckwit. If you're going to make your move it's now or never. We've got about ten minutes of taxi time left and then it's over so work it out, William. What are you thinking, Margaret? Get over it. He's not interested. He mustn't be interested. Just forget it.

Think about something else.

William

I could probably lean across and just rest my arm around her shoulders but she looks so shitty you know . . . she really looks aggro sitting there in the far corner of the cab as if she wants to kill me.

Margaret

This is just a fucking farce.

William

I can do this. I can do this. I can just . . .

33

Margaret

Fuck Fuck Fuck. My cunt is so wet.

William

— That's a new Kentucky Fried. How long has that been there?

Margaret

Forget it. Just forget it. It was a stupid idea. Forget it.

William

I figure when I get home I might give K. a ring. Like you know . . . the Margaret-thing was really attractive and all but if it's not going to pan out and just sort of peter out into nothing it at least served the purpose of reawakening a sort of . . . I don't know. I really could love you, Margaret. This is a shame. I wish it could have been otherwise. She and I could have really had a shot at this.

Margaret

What a shame.

William

Bummer.

Margaret

Bummer.

William

Pox as.

Margaret

This is pox.

Margaret

He's here. Lying beside me.

When we arrived at my house in Glen Waverley he saw me to the door while the taxi man sat and waited and pressed his buttons. As we stood on the porch, under the glow of the sensor-activated light, he set his hands gently upon my cheeks and stared at me, silent and still, perhaps struggling with some inner demons or self-censors or tummy grumbles or whatnots, and then with his fingers he scratched and scrunched some invisible beard I had apparently grown. This is finally it, I thought. Then after a long sigh, and a frown of melancholy regret, he gave the cheekiest and most annoying cocky, cock-sucking wink I've ever seen.

And then he left and the taxi drove him off and into the dark.

As I fumbled around the kitchen and made myself a hot chocolate, my little sister slobbed into my company, her hair all mussed from restless sleep, rubbing crumbs from her slumber-raggled eyes. She is at that point of an evening when people look their most dreadful, haggard and bewildered, at best startled and bemused, and she looks desperately beautiful.

Jane is fifteen years old and she has always been the most magnificent person I have ever seen. She has a mystical beauty. She is an unearthly and divine creature. I think perhaps that when the first faerie laughed for the first time, its laugh broke into a thousand pieces and one of those pieces became Jane. I hate her for it.

She is a perfect little missy, but the glory of her appearance conceals a sly and cunning temperament. I pour her a hot chocolate and we sit up at the breakfast bar, our legs folded up beneath ourselves, blowing our hot chocolates and warming our hands, clutching firmly to the mugs. She asks:

— How did tonight go?

— Good. I was wonderful.

— You were wonderful the two nights I saw you. I'm not surprised.

— Thanks, but tonight I was really wonderful.

— Maybe you should think about doing it seriously.

— Do you really think I could be a full-time actor?

— No. I mean prostitution. Maybe you should be a full-time hooker.

— Ha Ha, I say half-heartedly, and then we sit in silence for a few moments and address ourselves to our hot chocolates. Jane has sipped hers too far, and has given herself a cocoa-milky moustache that would look absurd on any other person. She says:

— Was Mister Wonderful there?

— Yep.

— Did he go to the cast party like you had planned?

— Kind of . . .

— Well, did he?

— Yes. Ish.

— Did you fuck him?

— Jane!!

— Well, did you kiss him?

— It's none of your business.

— Well did he at least tit you off?

— God you're gross!! Get away from me, dreadful child.

— Oh dear. No sex for Margaret-Shmargaret. Never mind. There's cucumbers in the crisper.

— You are just shocking, Janey. P.S. at least I've got my pleasant memories of sex.

— Ha Ha.

— I'm going to bed, I say, and unfold myself from the kitchen stool, and she leans up concurrently and kisses me on the cheek.

I turn off the lights as I pass through the house and walk up the two flights of stairs to my bedroom, checking that the heater is off at the switch and tiptoeing past my parents' bedroom on the first landing, and then up to my bedroom at the top. I fumble around, about to find the light switch but before I light the room I . . . sense something wrong. Something's not right, there's . . . I can feel that something's wrong in the room. Someone is here in my room. My heart is pounding like stones shaken in a tin bucket and I could scream but for the fact that my sound has been stolen and slain. I am trapped and ensnared by the legacy and testimony of a thousand novels I have read and films I have seen and news reports I have witnessed where thousands of women have been faced in thousands of cold dark rooms by thousands of murderers and psychopaths and rapists armed with knives and machetes and a thousand honed-down knitting needles. Shaking and terrified, I fumble with the light switch, ready and poised to back out and run for my soul down the stairs.

CLICK.

William is sitting at the foot of my bed, inhaling steadily from a marijuana water-pipe, and when I enter the room he looks up through his fringe and acknowledges me without breaking his concentration, or consumption of the dreaming smoke. He finishes and looks up from the pipe; his cheeks are full and he looks like a patient ailed by the mumps, and then he moves over to the open window and, with fitting concern for myself and for the sensitivities of my parents, he exhales the smoke out into the dark in one constant cloud.

He has walked some leaves of a tree into the bedroom and I think, It is so naughty of him not to wipe. With further thought, I conclude that it is actually very naughty of him to break into my house and bedroom and am about to chide him on the matter when he moves up close to me, having repacked the cone, kisses me on the nose and then grazes his dry lips slowly up and then off my fore-head (I think I made myself very cheap by inclining my face towards him), and offers me the bong.

It is sometime later and he's here. Lying beside me. His big hairy arms folded around my body, and one hand resting warmly between my legs, the knobbled joint of his thumb pressing almost imperceptibly, but pleasantly, against the lips and folds of my vagina. He is an earnest lover. I'll pay him that. But it is the earnestness of the unsure and the incompetent; the child actor cast as an adult in the school play, and caught fumbling nervously with the pockets and zips and folds of the oversized costume.

But he is sweet and earnest, as I say, and he generously and with great endeavour (but hopelessly) performed oral sex upon me for some twenty–twenty-five minutes, which I contentedly received, and feigned appreciation with crocodile moans and crocodile groans. His heart is in the right place, even if his tongue never was. And I do so like him. If this pans out (and I truly hope it does), I will have to soon explain to him the existence of my clitoris, and its precise location (second on the right and straight on till morning). There was something really strange that happened during the 'up and down as gaily as buckets in a well' bit of our sexual encounter. Something so par-ticular that during the post-coitus dreamy, slabby-dabby, mumbling-bumbly moments before we dozed off in each other's warm and sweet breath, I had to ask him about it, at the risk of destroying the precious moment and compromising his self-esteem:

— William. What was that you were saying when we were having sex?

— What?

— When you were speaking in French. While we were fucking?

— Oh . . . nothing really.

— Do you know much French?

— A bit. Well no . . . not a lot.

— Do you actually know what you said?

— Yes. Well no, actually.

— Oh.

— Well. What did I say?

— Nothing irregular.

— What was it?

— Nothing. It doesn't matter.

— No. Tell me.

— William . . .

— What? What did I say?

— You said, 'I love your milky white semen. Fill my three holes of virginity with your lovely cocks. You know how much I love it the most of all it is.'

All in all it wasn't that bad for a first-time fuck. No actually, I'll be honest here, it was pretty shocking. But he shows promise. We'll work it out.

William

This is wonderful.

I'm lying here beside Margaret.

I let the taxi take me just around the corner and then had him drop me off and I wandered back and sat for a while and watched the quiet and still house. I could have left it there, happy to just ponder this and that and unclaimed treasure and lost opportunities. But then . . . how can I say? I guess . . . odd things happen to us on our way through life without our noticing for a time that they have happened. This may well have been such a time. It was like Margaret and I were looming into each other's lives; like two stars that float through the dark and then shift into each other's orbit and then spin wildly around that same point, mutually attracted and repelled. I dearly wanted and needed this woman. There was this . . . like this great spiritual urgency and enormity and impetus to it, a great commotion in the firmament, and then the smallest of stars in the Milky Way screamed out: 'Now, William!'

I flew up to her window on the second floor, lying flat out on a strong wind that was going that way, and clicked open her window.

We shared a smoke and laughed at nothing, for quite some time, and then gave expression to the great love and attraction that we have both felt since she first came up to me and said, 'Excuse me. Can I ask whether you've read this book?'

I stood by her, rested my hands on her cheeks, watched and grazed and drank her in. I could have stood there forever, just entranced by how pretty and elegant and winsome and captivating and alluring and eminently fuckable she is. She looked up at me through her slightly squinting eyes, biting nervously on her bottom lip. She said:

— William, I am waiting.

— It's all very well to say you are waiting. So am I waiting.

— You're a cowardly custard.

— So are you a cowardly custard.

— I'm not frightened, William.

— Neither am I frightened.

— Well then, do it.

— Well, then you do it.

Then Margaret had a splendid idea.

— Why not both do it at the same time?

So at that same moment she inclined her face up to mine, and I cricked mine down towards her presented lips and closed eyes, and our mouths met at perhaps halfway and warmed each other's, both dry, but gradually softening to the touch of the other's. I was startled for a moment when I felt the slight pressure of her tongue eagerly nubbing and pressing against my lips, and then we collapsed into each other's lust. We said farewell to the surety of friendship and would now slowly and with uncertain paces map and chart the ravines and cliffs and traverses and treacherous landscapes of some kind of love.

Then I thimbled her.

She is lying next to me, curled with her back against me, asleep, and wheezing slightly.

Her breath is strong with garlic, not with the distasteful stench as might be exhaled from the mouth of the large hairy fellow who works at our petrol station and has a huge mole on his left cheek, or, and even not, in the sticky tepid way it might expire from the mouth and pores of the fairly attractive girl who catches the tram at my tram stop, and who has been reading *My Traitor's Heart* for about the last five months. But with a smug and warm confidence. Contented.

Her eyes are frosted with small crumbs of sleep, delicate little specks of slumber.

My hand rests between her legs, trembling slightly, cushioned snugly by her thighs, which a few hours earlier revealed themselves to be quite ample (she is slightly inclined to embonpoint), and cross-hatched by a network of fine, white stretch-marks that look like:

A. The rivers and waterways and tributaries mapped on a riverboat captain's charts.

B. The lines of white powder that we herd and group into columns on horizontal mirrors.

C. The spindly and gentle trails left by snails on wet pavements after a storm.

D. The white and cracked lines creased into the spine of a well-read paperback novel.

Happy, plump thighs, tacky and smeared with the remnants of my semen and saliva, and her vaginal fluids.

And we love going down on Margaret.

This is a woman pretty much tuned in and cool about the format and nature and structure of her own sexuality.

I love the way she hauls one leg up and over to mount and straddle my face, brazenly lowers herself down onto my mouth and tongue, and grinds herself into my face as I desperately flicker my lips and tongue against her cunt bone, her bearing down and chasing her orgasm.

43

It's fucking divine raunch.

None of this timid jittery-cunt thing that some women have got going.

I think perhaps this is the most wondrous and beautiful woman in all of Christiandom.

It was a great fuck. The best ever.

Margaret

Well, the next morning was a fucking disaster.

I overslept . . .

No actually, I don't believe that. I don't believe that I overslept at all. In any sane and reasonable world, and with any sane and reasonable person, I was sleeping on quite fairly. I would have eventually woken up at a fitting time, fumbled my way out of sleep, and stretched and flexed my legs and toes, and then with some short panic realised the presence of a person next to me, registered their identity, fucked them, and then smuggled them out of the house after my mother and father had left to go to work.

Instead, I was jolted out of sleep by a loud yelp I immediately identified as that of a stupid and ungainly pooch that has a particularly small and defenceless rabbit under its control and dependent on its whim. After a few moments of further consideration I recognised it as my sister's usual and chilling response to anything that causes her particular delight. Startled, I logged on to my surroundings and circumstances as quickly as possible and was ahooten-shocked to register the absence of someone lying next to me in my bed. This should not have struck me as irregular. My parents are not of a liberal temperament such that they allow me to 'entertain' young male friends overnight in my bed, so the circumstances of waking in the morning to the absence of a person in my bed beside me is, by an overwhelming majority, that of the norm. However, on this particular morning I should have been waking up to the absence of a person lying in the bed beside me at the same time as I should not have been waking up to the absence of a person asleep in the bed beside me. I quickly threw on some track-and-field pants and a windcheater, and with some fitting excess of trepidation, trudged down the stairs to the kitchen. There I was greeted by an unnerving tableau: my mother and father, in various stages of workaday dress, standing slightly addled and unsure of themselves, my little sister perched up on one of the kitchen stools in a T-shirt and some small blue and white knickers, drinking in the scene with all the joy of a particularly malicious Puck, and in their midst the cause of their either distressed or delighted state, my new lover, a jug of juice in one hand, and clad only in my white terry-towelling dressing-gown—the pink rose-buds detailed on the collar floating prettily around his thick and hairy neck, the front loose and open, the lazily tied cord barely bringing the gown together to conceal his genitals.

Silence.

My mother and father both turned to me with eyes befuddled and mouths agape, Jane looked up at me and again yelped with overflowing delight, and William saluted me with the jug of juice in his hand and, oblivious to the stress and situation of which he was the cause and epicentre, observed innocently:

— Yum. Tropical Fruit Crush.

Bewildered silence.

— Get upstairs and get dressed you idiot, I say and then move into the kitchen and take the juice from him, having to push him into motion as he is standing shy-struck, his face looking all so confused and his feelings hurt by the harshness of my tone.

An excess of bewildered silence.

A few moments pass and then my father disappears also, not to perform any particular duty or function but to avoid

46

any in the looming and inevitable conversation. After he has left my mother quietly and with faltering speech that gradually strengthens with confidence says:

— Well . . . Margaret. I think that . . . you owe us an explanation.

— Can we not have this conversation?

— We certainly will have this conversation, young lady.

— Look, nothing happened. He saw me home and didn't have money for a cab home so he crashed on the floor upstairs. Nothing happened.

— Nothing happened, my sister echoes, with stage irony. I say:

— Piss off, Jane.

— Don't you talk to your sister like that. You know the rules. Your father and I cannot do anything about how you behave when you leave this house but while you are under this roof . . .

— Look. I cannot do this now. Let's not fucking . . .

— Margaret!! That's enough of that language.

The fight continues by this manner and in this manner until such time as it is interrupted by the reappearance of William, more suitably clad but no more welcome as he shuffles sheepishly into the kitchen and presses his back against the fridge, his sweaty palms clasping against it nervously sending the fridge magnets, telephone bills, shopping notes, photographs and video library cards falling noisily to the floor. He says:

— Hi . . . I'm um . . . William. I'm sorry if I . . . He trails off hopelessly.

— William, this is my mother and you met my father before . . . This is my sister Jane.

She crosses her two index fingers and without a word raises them at William. Despite my better judgment I wearily ask her why:

— Why did you do that? Why did you go and do the Dracula-cross thing?

— Because William is evil. Because he is the spawn of the devil.

— Jane, what are you doing?

— He's the bastard that got Andrea Stone pregnant.

My mother yells:

— Jane!! That's enough. We've got a difficult enough situation here as it is without you stirring everyone up.

— That's what one of the nuns said. She said he is a window through which the devil can reach into this family and destroy us all.

William says:

— I'm actually not really a window for the devil, you know.

— No. I know. I heard you were a bit of a loser, actually.

— I'm sort of halfway between the two.

I interrupt their discourse:

— William, you'll have to excuse my little sister if she behaves badly occasionally. She's still a virgin.

— I am not a virgin!!

My mother interjects with alarm:

— Jane!!

— Okay. I am. I am. I'm a virgin all right. Just chill out, okay.

My father returns, fumbling with his briefcase, and before I have a chance to speak Jane pipes in:

— This is Papa Bear. Papa Bear, this is the father of your first grandchild. He usually shoots through pretty soon so we won't be seeing him again.

— God you're a suck, Jane. Can you just go off and teen suicide or something. And close your legs, you little tart.

Dad backs me up:

— You are being a suck, Jane. And go and get dressed. Hello, William. I'm disappointed by what's happened here

48

but I don't see why we can't all work towards making the best of a bad situation.

He shakes William's hand and kisses my sister and mother farewell. He nods a stern goodbye to me but then relents and kisses me reassuringly on the forehead. With a propensity for doing the wrong thing and saying the wrong thing in any difficult circumstance, William looks up to him hopefully and asks:

— Where are you off to? Is there any chance you can give me a lift close to town?

Dad turns away from him with no answer, his bustle and manner now suggesting an opinion of dislike that he was formerly prepared to reserve. He grumbles up the hall and slams the door behind him. Those of us remaining stand in silence until I throw the jug of juice over William and leave the room. Jane yelps with delight.

William

I really can't remember that well the first time I met Margaret's family.

I think it was a bit of a disaster.

I think her dad had a moustache.

I seem to remember it being in the morning for some reason.

Her little sister is an exceedingly beautiful person, with a lithe and sinewy body and the healthy grassy gamin presence of a tall girl knocking on the door of womanhood. She has short dark hair the colour of a raven's feathers (a particularly black raven, who has flown through a hill of coal dust and fallen in a barrel of ink and been caught in an oil slick on a moonless night, called 'Sooty') and it is neatly gathered forward, framing her elegant face. She has dark and sullen mocking eyes and her skin has the colour and nature of cobwebs: glowing dully and translucent, and it begs and demands to be touched, so that one may ascertain whether she is indeed cool and made of ice or whether she is warm and waxy and textured like a pearl.

She was wearing a T-shirt that had a zeppelin and the word 'AERONEF' on the front, and just to the right of the airship, which was slightly distorted by her pert small but firm and well proportioned breasts that were rising up and pressing warmly against the T-shirt fabric, and near her right armpit were three small holes as if the T-shirt had caught on something and she'd dragged it; and she was wearing a small pair of knickers that had pale blue and white stripes running across them horizontally and every second blue stripe was slightly darker and they had lace running across the top but the side elastic that came around her legs wasn't as elaborately laced but still you could see there'd been a bit of work gone into it and it was a slightly lemon colour and on the inside of her left leg there was a bit of cotton that had come a bit unravelled and if you licked your fingers you could twirl it into a pin-like spear which you could then pull out but there's the chance that in doing so you might then unravel the material further so it would probably be better if you put your mouth to the hem of her knickers and got the stray thread between your teeth and ground away at it gently until it severed and I could see where the mass of her pubic hair was causing a bit of a rise, a slight hump in the fabric of her knickers and if you looked really closely you could see three stray hairs poking out from the side of her right leg where she had a birthmark in the shape of an upside-down Africa and it even had a smaller supplementary birthmark lying beside it in the place where Madagascar is and her bum cheeks were leaving a smeary sweaty mark on the vinyl upholstered stool she was sitting on and later on when she left the room and I put my hand on the seat it still felt warm and damp and sweet.

Margaret

That was the manner by which William and I commenced our affair and though he returned to the house for a few official functions and occasions, his relationship with my parents was never repaired. I spend as much time, and the greater part of my time, around at William's house, a large and many roomed, three-storey terrace house in Carlton which he shares with six other lazy, listless, indolent and like-minded young men, which results in successive and protracted arguments with my parents, with no sign of them relenting on the issue. I storm up to my bedroom and slam doors and shout profanities and then William appears at my window and whisks me out and into the dark.

On one particular evening when he arrived on the understanding that my parents were attending a function at No. 27, he boldly and confidently bounced up to the front door, happily rapped out 'Shave-and-a-Haircut Bop Bop' on the knocker and then was terror-struck by the presentation of my father opening the door, having had his departure delayed by a prolonged battle with a particularly difficult and displeasing necktie that would not allow itself to be secured successfully around his neck. His surly suggestion that William depart was met by William's heartfelt entreaty that he at least be allowed a word with me, which was answered with a negative and which was countered by another plea, and so they would have stood there for the whole evening had I not sailed furiously down the stairs, advised my father that he was 'A Fucking Cunt' and when my mother emerged from the kitchen extended the compliment to her also, and then, running from the house and dragging William by the hand behind me, I forswore ever returning to, or living in, the house again.

William and I drove away and to his home, the music on the radio screaming at us to either turn around and drop me back, or alternatively, to keep on driving and past William's house and on and up forever (it all depended on which way you listened to it). We shouted at each other over the noise, screeching and singing along, spilling beers and passing a joint between us, nipping food out of the mouths of eagles and flying close to the water and touching sharks' tails as we passed. Laughing at nothing and throwing empty cans out of the windows, setting fire to ourselves with dropped cigarettes (always funny that one), racing through red lights and screaming past the stars and bumping our heads against the clouds. We dumped what few items I had deemed necessities in his room, shared three mild joints and a couple of lines ('For no one can fly unless the faerie dust has been blown on him') and then went out on a pub crawl, hooting and shrieking from hotel to hotel, fighting and laughing and crying without discrimination with sundry strangers and assorted friends. William, to his great delight, was able to cause three fights at once in one particular pub, and the matter was confused by the fact that in the middle of a fight he would suddenly change sides. Concurrently, I was having a brawl with a woman in the female toilets over a particular, half-empty, glass of scotch that we both claimed as our own, and which was later revealed to belong to neither of us. The rightful owner had her nose broken against the side of a toilet bowl by the two previous combatants in an encouraging display of bipartisan collaboration. At another pub William was courted by an amazingly beautiful transvestite called Tiger Lily (they so often look so very, very beautiful; I think because they spend two hours rendering themselves female whereas we spend a split second), and I by a very handsome model who had once appeared in 'Neighbours'.

By the time the drugs and alcohol began to wear off we found ourselves feeling tired and wretched in the centre of town; a couple of seedy and sick strays standing in a cold drizzle, and buffeted by a shitful cold wind, and with absolutely no means of transport home. We climbed the scaffolding and ladders that adorned the facade of the Melbourne Town Hall as it underwent restoration, and then made aimless and scattered love in the high clock tower surrounded by the pigeon shit and the dirt and the rubbish and the stars and the quiet wheeze of the sleeping city.

The next morning we sheepishly climbed back down the scaffolding, pale and desperately unwell, made our apologies to the amused work-persons and pissed off home.

William

Margaret smells; and that's a factor.

She doesn't stink, and she's not distasteful to inhale but rather, look it's like this: there are always two means by which one can arrive at any middle point. If we use the example of say a colour spectrum, one can get from blue to yellow in two ways. We can by gradually shifting from special blue through the murky fog of varying hues of green until we emerge into the sunlight of crisp yellow. Or alternatively we can strip back the blue, filter it and filter it, until we come to white, and then from that white we build our yellow in increasing lustrous powders till we achieve our refined egg-yolk yellow. Similarly it has been said of a particular friend of mine that he is halfway between heterosexual and homosexual, without meaning that he's bisexual (the figurative equivalent of our green), but rather that he's non-sexual or ambi-sexual or kind-of-not-anything-and-yet-something-sexual, an essential and pure white on which one can add hues of blue or shades of yellow according to one's reflective position. Some people are right wing and some people are left wing and some people have figured out their political beliefs and are halfway between the two. And some people have never thought about it and don't have a disposition either way. Some people love rhinos and hate zebras, and others love zebras and hate rhinos, and some people just figure that both animals have their good qualities and their bad. And some people, well all they can think about is chickens. Chicken-this and chicken-that, just chickens chickens chickens.

The point being that Margaret smells but she doesn't stink.

Some people don't smell. Not of perfume and not of odour. They just don't smell.

Smell-less.

That is their median.

Middle.

White.

Margaret achieved this same median not through absence of smell but by bringing two conflicting forces to zero-point; her basic and essential body odour is constantly in conflict with the scents and perfumes that she uses to disguise that natural odour. She finely balances the smell of vagina and sweat, and arse and armpit stench and staleness with its counterpart in the smell of deodorant, perfume and scented spray.

The effect is joyous.

An exhilarating cocktail of essence and artifice, truth and falsity, faeces and facade.

This is quite lovely.

She is real.
I can taste the person/poison.
Under the dressing.
She lives.

Now her little sister Jane?
Jane doesn't smell.
She is a goddess.
Jane doesn't go to the toilet or pass wind or have period cramps.
I think perhaps what happens is she goes to sleep in the evening and then by morning a small pink sachet of lavender-scented waste matter has appeared on her bed-side table. And then perhaps two bluebirds appear and flutter in through the window and, chuckling to them-selves—over some barely remembered joke or riddle, the punchline alone being enough to send themselves both into paroxysms of laughter (something as innocent as 'But I ordered cheese with this!!' or 'In-deed!!') and it takes them some minutes to regain their composure—and these two bluebirds take the two ties of ribbon, which seal the small Laura Ashley package, in their beaks and fly it out through the windows surrounded by butterflies and beams of sunlight and rainbows and a particularly colourful, though slightly verbose, toucan, across fields of golden wheat populated by singing and dancing curtain-clad Von Trapp children.
I think perhaps that's the way Jane Palmer disposes of waste matter.
Because she is an angel.

I shit.
I shit lots.
Horrible stringy splatters of mustard-coloured paste that fall and spray the inside of the bowl.

I remember the neat little cakes I used to pass as a child.
Neat, compact buns of chocolate-coloured poo.
'Poops.'
That was before great quantities of beer and too many cigarettes and before I took control of my own diet.
Now?
Well it just doesn't bear thinking about.

Margaret

Living with William and the boys is an awfully big adventure.

We have very little money, the boys being unemployed, and largely unemployable, and the only steady income is from their unemployment benefits and the not considerable money that William brings home from the bookshop. His job, tenuously held though it is, does at least give him some status in the house, and they are happy to follow his directives on most issues, to accord him the respect of father-figure and breadwinner, and to willingly resell all the books he steals from the shop to various second-hand bookstores.

There is amongst them the occasional outburst of intense and industrious activity, and this is to be admired and encouraged. During these spasmodic explosions of commerce they will awaken at a reasonable hour, shower and shave, and go off to pursue their enterprise: to shoplift, pilfer and thieve. In the evenings they return from their adventures, like proud hunters, with hundreds of pocket-size goods—hair-clips and hole-punchers, compasses and tins of sardines, intriguing paperweights and packets of blank audio cassettes, small boxes of Lego and sprinkler attachments. Never anything that could be of any value to any person that has ever lived and ever been, ever. They will then spread this booty out on the kitchen table (a door set on what seems to be a two-foot tree-trunk), with all the flourish of a slightly sinister Arab merchant unfolding his blanket to reveal precious rubies and jewels and artefacts from The East.

I think they are all just a wee bit buffle-headed.

As the evening progresses, and the beer is drunk and the dope is smoked, the stories of their adventures in claiming these items become more outrageous and embellished; the chihuahua that yapped at their heels as they stole the sprinkler-timer becomes a blue heeler that bit their arm and then later a doberperson that took a big chunk out of their thigh, and by the evening's end, a wolf that made off with one of their accomplices.

Occasionally one of them will be a bit bold and take William to task on his bourgeois values and sensibilities in having a regular and conventional job, to which he replies slightly disdainfully and with great alacrity, 'It's not a job. It's just a place I go to to steal books and stationery, and to pick up chicks', and he'll look across the table at me and give me a conspiratorial wink.

Actually, the more I think about them, these lost boys, and think about the way they behave, the more I figure they are a tribe of idiots.

One of them is a bass guitarist in a rock band that in fact disbanded three years previously, but the rest of the band has never had the heart to tell him since he's pinned so much on their eventual success at breaking into the Japanese market. And so they meet with him every four weeks or once a month, and jam with him for an hour, and then they disappear back to their more reasonable lives. He feels guilty because he's thinking of dropping out because they just aren't getting any gigs, but he doesn't want to 'let the guys down'.

Another is a playwright, who has written one play in the four years of his career, and which will never be performed because for all its good qualities and interesting character development, it requires one performer to change costume eighteen times in half an hour, a person in a rhinoceros costume who can ride a unicycle and, at the play's conclusion, fresh fish to be thrown at the audience.

A third, Shane or Sam or Michael or something, has taken out the copyright on all combinations and permutations of the terms 'Mac' and 'Vegie' and 'Veg' and 'Vegetable' and 'Burger' in the belief that one day a certain multinational restaurateur will catch up with certain culinary trends and then come knocking on his door with chequebook in hand.

Another is an untrained chef who is convinced that his idea about pickling onions in raspberry vinegar will make him his fortune.

They are fools; happy fools. Sweet and innocent and endearing fools. And they are a constant delight. But they are fools.

Get-rich-quick schemes abound.

One of them has a dope plant in the laundry, trying hard to grow in the centre of the room, and he hopes that when it blooms to its full potential he can then enter the exciting world of low-level drug dealing, but the plant is constantly trimmed and pruned by the other boys and never grows above two feet.

For a time they had a thriving and comparatively successful industry. The days would be spent abducting any stray cats or dogs or other motley pets loose in the neighbouring streets and alleys, or tethered and encaged in rear gardens, and these were quartered in the backyard and garage until such time as a 'Lost and Reward' notice would appear in the local milk bar. Then one or other of the boys would return the animal to its owner to be greeted with heartfelt thanks and the reward: ten or fifteen dollars, and other sundry items—a couple of bottles of beer, jars of jam or discount coupons to various retail outlets. On one occasion the return of a particularly hefty tabby cat was rewarded with a dozen freshly baked coconut cookies made by the cat's co-tenant ('One very small old lady with a hooked nose'), and so well were these cookies enjoyed by all that the woman's cat 'went missing' another five times that fortnight, until such time as her suspicions led to the police visiting the house and the enterprise was abandoned.

As they were all receiving a minimal amount from the government by way of unemployment relief, the finances of the house were tightly strictured; however, they made do by some means. I guess essentially they survived by ruthlessly striking out any extravagances and frivolous purchases, and reserving their money for what were considered necessities. In this house the extravagances were deemed to be food and healthy sustenance and the necessities proved to be ample quantities of alcohol and mind-altering drugs.

Another regular event that punctuated their calendar was the six-weekly raid upon one or other's parents' home. One of them would head off sadly in the morning and would catch the train to the outlying eastern suburbs, or be driven in a car borrowed for the occasion, and from there they'd see themselves into the parental home and greedily scavenge food from their parents' pantries or refrigerators. Useless food: tins of lychees and creamed corn, whole baby beets and Selza Saline (LEMON FLAVOUR Glucose Enriched—375 g net).

On one particular and black occasion, Curly mistimed his pantry-raid to correspond with his only sister's 21st birthday, and he had to spend an hour or so sitting and talking with various aunts and great-aunts, and joins senile

Uncle Sasha in a one-hour diatribe against the corn traders of Vlissingen, while the other six sat in a brown mini out the front, pulled up to the kerb, stoned and laughing and singing and angrily honking the horn.

Early on in my time there I volunteer a pantry-raid upon my own parents' home and my nocturnal foray was interrupted by Jane sleepily stumbling down the stairwell and into the kitchen (me stoned and with half a dozen cans of randomly selected food and a light globe and a cat called Missy Missy Missy clutched to my laugh-heaving breast), and her saying, 'Boy, are you in the shit-books or what'.

I never hear mention of any of the boys having girlfriends or particular female friends. Sporadically my visits to the bathroom have me meeting some other woman; peering into the mirror and smearing my lipstick onto her chin, or patting my deodorant under her arms, but whether these were actual girlfriends or occasional lovers could be subject to dispute. More frequently than stands to be considered as coincidence, they are other drug-fucked souls who had mistaken our house for their own.

Birthdays are a particular boon; and this one or the other one's cheque from his parents or a grandmother or a wealthy aunt would be committed to the house 'kitty', and entrusted to that particular one of them who was best poised to purchase drugs economically at that especial moment.

We do seem to get shit-faced quite frequently, the boys sitting up and amusing each other and boring each other witless as the moment and contraband see fit; and William and I retiring to our room, nodding and giggling our 'sleep wells and goodnights'. Smiling stupidly at each other, or laughing without cause, or gently tracing our dry, cracked fingers across the other's shivering naked body, detailing and circling this particular freckle or mole or blemish, or forcefully thrusting each other up against the wall. He would let his cloak slip softly to the ground, and then biting his lip till a lewd blood stood on them. I, crawling naked up across the dishevelled sheets of our sex-stained bed, bent over and looking through my legs in a way that would defy and frighten wolves. And then we'd crash into each other's lust, picking and scratching and biting the very cause and source from the other one's life; trying to find that one elusive bit of the other that we could never quite claim. And fuck and sweat and roar our way through towards the morning. We'd lie and graze our fingers across each other's forehead, snuggling into the sweat drying cold on the other one's arms; drinking in the miasma of the night.

In that first week after the 'Function at No. 27' night, Jane called a couple of times and my father called and my mongrel mother paid hundred and two hundred dollar lots into my bank account and then we treated ourselves with particularly fine speed and some remarkably good ABA tabs. I love living in this crazy, listless, hyperactive house and I will thrive in this house where we unknowingly trek mud in and onto the carpet. Where we sluggishly stagger out of bed at midday or at noon and passionately argue the points raised on Oprah or Sally or Phillip. Where each fart is celebrated and each burp is considered and compared and assessed, and where each crashing body blundering through the kitchen and out into the backyard is applauded for the quantity and quality of vomit they retch into the soil. Where we scream at each other and fight with each other, and give each other's chin a loving bite, and then happily crash into each other's arms and love and fuck each other filthy.

I am home.

61

I can only stand living there for three weeks before the smell and the dirt and the shiftless inanity of it all becomes too much to bear. So I return home, greeted by the marked relief and silent recriminations of my parents and the wide-eyed attention of my sister, to renourish and recuperate, and then will return again to William and his childish heaven. By this way I maintain two homes and two lives, shifting from the stability and good food and health of suburbia, and then masked in my alter-ego I slime off to the grunge and grime of the inner city and the outer world.

William

Margaret leaves traps for me.

Not tricks or stratagems to ensnare and endanger me, but rather, booby traps of delight, left around my bedroom and our house. Little 'Margaretisms' that she has, without thought, left for me to discover.

At some point during the day I'll be performing some menial task and encounter a domestic irregularity that reminds me of her wonderful presence in my life.

Blundering and bumbling into the kitchen some time after her departure, I'll open a cupboard to find that the bag of breakfast cereal has been folded over and fastened with a clothes peg.

I don't do that.

None of the other boys do that.

That's something that someone else has done. 'Oh. My Margaret.'

There are elastic bands appearing on the door handles (a good place to keep them and I'll be buggered if I would have remembered where I would have put them), and sealing the plastic on half-eaten bricks of cheese. Cakes of soap are being unwrapped and appearing on the shelves and nooks of the bathroom, where they can await use and additionally scent the air.

On a more remedial level, dirty clothes are rendezvousing in the wash basket, wet towels are being hung on the backs of chairs or on the towel rail (at last, a use for it has been found), and toilet paper rolls are being fitted to the toilet roll holder, as opposed to just sitting vertically upon it. (Why do slob bachelors never fit their toilet paper to the toilet paper holder? Do we really save that much time?)

In this way, and throughout the day, I will happen upon a different indicator of her recent presence (How come all the empty beer cans are in the bin? Why are all the ashtrays empty? Whose great idea was it to put the bread in the freezer?), and with the recognition of their source, I feel all googly-woogly inside.

Who is this delightful woman?

How wonderful are the incidences of her ways?

And who could not love a woman who leaves the knife sitting in the pot with the boiling vegetables only so that in a few moments time it will be easier to then slice the butter.

And there is a bra.

A curled black bra.

A bra that has somehow wandered up the broken path to our front porch, opened the door or stolen in through a window, crept or slithered up the hallway, and settled on the floor of my bedroom.

Either that or Margaret has left it here.

And why?

Why did she one day leave without a bra?

Or that previous night come with two?

Because it is our bra.

Hers and mine.

William's and Margaret's.

And it lives at my house because we're a couple.

Hers to make use of in some emergency—as our departure from the house is delayed by the untimely breakage (?) of the bra she is wearing; the pleasures of the evening are suddenly endangered but, 'No. Fear not. We have a spare.'

And mine to hold and clutch to me when I sleep alone, to sedate myself with the smug aroma of her talcum powder which has infiltrated the fabric, to luxuriate in the pleasure of its silky texture against my coarse chest.

To occasionally regard and consider, turning it slowly in my fingers, like Hamlet with his skull, or Joseph Banks with some new and remarkable strain of flora, or more directly, like some particular fellow who has in his possession a stray undergarment that belongs to the woman he loves.

She is a delight.

She is a constant delight.

Every moment of my life is so much greater, the sky so much bluer, the wind that more temperate, the trees that bit more tree-ish because she is a part of me.

Here's another thing that I consider to be grouse about Margaret.

She presses the nose on her cat to find out whether it's cold outside.

About a weekend ago we slept at her place because her parents and her sister were down at their beach house. (Now that's always fun. Since I've been a grown-up my months of tedium and poverty are often punctuated by these visits to this or that girlfriend's parents' house and for a weekend or a week I delight in the access to proper food and clean carpets and the comfort of their bed. We sit in their warm dressing-robes and watch videos on their wide-screen televisions. We have proper meals on proper and uniform crockery and sneak sly glances at ourselves enjoying this glimpse of the type of decorous middle-class Darby and Joan we could have been. I hope that parents appreciate the delight that their young offspring take in their absence; that for those few days we play at being a well and correct and a clean and cosy couple, like dwarfish thieves in giant robes.) One morning, on this weekend spent at the Palmers' house, we woke up and Margaret called her cat, 'Missy Missy Missy', and her cat pushed its way in through the window and she gently pressed her finger against its nose to see how cold its nose was, and therefore, how cold it was outside. And so she would plan her wardrobe accordingly.

Like, excuse me, I think that's mega-cute.

Isn't that endearing.

Isn't that pulchritudinous.

I think so.

I think she's a wonder.

And before we move on can we all just momentarily acknowledge the fact that 'pulchritudinous' is a pretty remarkable word, and to save you the distraction of having to quickly refer to your dictionary, it means beautiful.

I think it means beautiful.

Either that or it's the name of that dinosaur who looked a bit like a Triceratops, with the frills and everything, but who didn't have horns but just had this beak-like nose. You know the fellow. Pulchritudinous Rex.

By the way, while we're on this point, were dinosaurs ever women? Can you sort of picture a girl dinosaur? I know they must have been because they layed eggs and had sex (Isn't that a thought?) and stuff like that but really, don't they just seem like a whole lot of blokes hanging

65

around for a couple of million years and doing blokish stuff like fighting and pissing and running away from volcanoes and eating trees and stuff?

I reckon they do. I reckon they do a lot.

Point being, I like Margaret.

I like her so much.

I really do.

She can be funny, delightful, boring and angry and gnarly but hell my life is made that little bit richer for having her in it.

And it's nice to know that someone else has thought 'my life is a bit the better if William Casey's there'.

That's a pretty good thing too.

We love Margaret.

We'll keep her.

II

'The hateful telling broke out again.'

Peter Pan
J.M. Barrie

After a time, and as we grew, we stopped playing at being Aunt Peggy, and started asking about her. We never asked our Grandmother, it was sort of known not to. We asked our parents, but they didn't know the full story either. It was a long time ago.

'I never really knew the full story,' they'd say. 'It was a long time ago.'

Actually, in the end we did ask our Grandmother.

My cousin Sandra lost weight, and gained impertinence, and asked our Grandmother what happened with Aunt Peggy.

First Aunt Peggy has to disappear suddenly. Twice.

Their farm of stones was near a town, which had no name, and about thirty miles on was another town called Galverston and there was no road to Galverston. There was a train line. On the train they took automobile parts to Galverston, and there they assembled cars and drove them around.

Around Galverston. It was an island on an island.

Great Aunt Peggy walked to the nameless town and got a lift with the postman on the postman's cart near to Galverston and then caught the train and by this means and that she arrived in Launceston, a major town on the Northernmost coast of Neverland. She had left a mass of washing just sitting on the kitchen table. Just like that!! Just up and left!!

My Grandmother's family followed Peggy and left the farm near the unnamed town and went to Launceston. My Grandmother and her mother and the wordless man followed with the rest of the family; four other girls and a boy called 'Boy'. They lumbered and loomed after the eldest daughter on an ox-drawn wagon. In Launceston they saw a tank that had been used in the First World War, and met an aunty with a small dead twin joined to her hip. She called it 'The Little Dolly' and washed it and combed its hair and decorated it with lipstick and powder. She would ask my Grandmother whether she'd like to kiss 'The Little Dolly' and would hold my Grandmother by the back of her head and force her face up against the small, withered dead child. My Grandmother would scream and cry.

They rented a house on Wellington Street and Aunt Peggy was folded back within the family and there the young girl was to have been buried; obeying the oldest and attending to the youngest. But now she had learnt how to peek and slip out and away from under the heavy pleats and folds of her mother's austere dresses, away from under her father's stern and sharply starched working clothes, and out from behind the mass of sundry torn and grass-stained skirts and shirts of her sisters and Boy.

Great Aunt Peggy watched with wonder the trolley-cars that bustled down the centre of the wide streets and was wholly atickled by the ladies' hats and shawls and ribbons and laughed with delight and joy at the antics and ribald humour of the young men who followed her home from where she worked in the hospital laundry.

The wordless fellow worked with the railways and was away for twelve days and then home for a weekend as he and his workmates inched the train lines further and further into Neverland.

His wife sewed at night for the neighbours and baked through the day and played at cards with Mrs Cookson from over on Vernon Street.

My Grandmother was beaten by the nuns because she was slow to learn her catechism, was bitten by a black dog that lived down below the bakery, and knocked out three of her teeth with the head of an axe (accidentally).

Boy swapped his boxing gloves with Rob Mullins for a magic lantern, swapped the magic lantern for Alf Mason's paper round, and gave the paper round to Black Murphy's brother in exchange for a fishing net with four floats.

Aunt Peggy climbed in through windows late at night and roused my Grandmother from her bed to dance. She sung while she changed the beds and hummed while she beat the mats and whistled when she wiped down the wainscot. She smiled at and teased the boys with the askew-whiff caps and let them hold her hand as they walked her along the Tamar River, and sat with her legs swinging slightly as they shared fish and chips on a bench down by the bridge, and stood shyly in their bed-sits, twirling and entwining her fingers in the black lace that edged the cuffs of her sleeves, and waited as they hastily made their rooms presentable, throwing idle socks and stray newspapers and miscellaneous ties in a pile in the corner. She lowered her eyes and timidly looked up from behind her fringe, and smiled appreciatively as they opened with great ceremony a cheap bottle of pungent and keenly distressing wine.

And then suddenly, and perhaps after six or seven months, my Great Aunt Peggy disappeared. She left Launceston and Neverland and caught the great boat to the mainland; turned at the first left and then on till the dark of night.

Great Aunt Peggy died.

She died in Melbourne on the mainland.

My mother's grandmother went to Melbourne to bring Aunt Peggy back to her home and to her family in Tasmania. Back to the pretty little house with the funny red walls and the mossy green roof, and the gay windows all about with roses peeping in.

She came back with a baby.

No Aunt Peggy.

A baby instead.

Baby Boo.

William

—How many lovers have you had? asks Margaret.
This is a bit that I'm thinking about at the moment.
This is a bit that matters.

Margaret and I have been going out for about six weeks
or two months or at least an extended period of time. They
have been blissful. We cannot find fault. I think we absolutely delight each other. And one wonders how long such
exquisite perfection can last. One watches for the trigger,
for the germ, for the bug or bruise that will spread the
infection that will turn cancerous that will kill the relationship. It happens in every relationship. The outbreak of the
hateful telling.

I dearly love Margaret.
I think she loves me.
Perhaps we are immune.

— How many lovers have you had? Margaret asks me,
her voice faltering and muffled as it comes at a distance
from behind the pillow I have scrunched up under myself,
clutching it to my face, and her voice further weakened
by the nodding sleepiness that threatens to overwhelm her.
We are lying together on my bed in the cobwebbed light
and gentle dreamy stupor that is characteristic and inseparable from a blissful, overcast autumn afternoon spent
inside in the warmth having sex; caught up and entangled
in the sheets and bedclothes and each other.

— How many lovers have you had?

— What? I ask by way of answer, knowing what she
said but giving her a chance to retreat from the question.
Allowing her enough time to consider the energy it will

involve for her to reconstitute and re-animate her face and mouth from the relaxed dropped cheeks and slightly downturned mouth and slackened jaw that follow the expression of any '-ad' word, to the comparatively exuberant and draining strength required to say any 'H-' word, the cheeks creased up in a crocodile grin, the tongue inactive, but still drainingly held up in the middle of the mouth, and the breath pressing numbly against the fore of the mouth, and the back of the teeth. The distance from '. . . had?' to 'How . . .' is quite considerable and I hope Margaret's endeavour and facial muscles are not up to the task because this is a conversation I fear and dread having.

— How many lovers have you had?

— Why do you ask?

— I don't know . . . I just was wondering.

— Well it doesn't matter, you know . . . more than a virgin and less than a whore, I guess. A few.

I'm not answering her question. And I'm not refusing to answer it. These things don't matter. It's not like we can scribe on paper two columns, and head one with the subject title 'Margaret's Lovers' and the other with 'William's Lovers' and then tick off one against the other and finish up with a surplus or deficit on the side of column A or column B. It's not as if her Adam Williamson will cancel out my Katherine Elizabeth Shanning and my Joy Carter will cancel out her Edward. These things always work out more damnably involved and contrived than that, and it only took me the experience of this retrospective recrimination on three prior occasions to realise that it ends with both partners being upset.

And yet I'm not saying 'Let's just drop it, okay.'

And I'm not saying 'Three' or 'Twenty-seven', or 'Eighty-six million', and leaving the matter at that.

So what am I doing?

I'm drawing it out.

I'm prodding her towards asking the question again, a third time, or a fourth.

I'm letting us be drawn into the conversation.

And I will answer eventually because yes, I want to know also.

I want to know how many lovers Margaret has had.

I want to know how many nameless men have held her in their arms.

I want to know how many nameless, faceless men can make the same claim to her as I can.

I want to know how many soulless, nameless, faceless men can make this same claim to her love and on her trust as I, and then I want to value it accordingly.

And that's fucked, but now she's asked we're both set on this course.

I want to know how many men have held Margaret, have kissed her sweating brow, have clutched the fine hair at the nape of her neck as they come. Have seen her lie before them and watched her draw her arms up above her body and set the palms of her hands against the wall at the head of the bed to steady her shifting body as she forces and grinds herself onto their cock. Have seen her straighten her arms by her side and force her breasts up and together as she eases herself open to receive them, have seen her look back, grinning slyly, over the one shoulder or the other, trying to catch their lips with hers as they frantically push themselves into her from behind, clasping and slapping and pressing open her arse cheeks and tracing the rise and fall of her spine with the backs of their nail-bitten fingers, and absentmindedly picking at the chocolate brown freckle on her left shoulder blade.

I want to torture myself. I want to destroy my soul.

There is no right number of previous lovers to have had.

It is one of those certainties of social and relationship mathematics that one's ex-lovers (X♥) will always be equal to 'the fitting and correct number of ex-lovers to have had' (X♥:✓), plus that one extra ex-lover who so wrenches and rends and tears apart your partner's love and heart (X♥=X♥:✓+1). And it doesn't matter whether X♥ equals one or seventeen or seventy-hundred, it is always made up of these two parts, the number of lovers that can be excused and accepted *plus* that one person whom one cannot reconcile oneself to; the bloke at the party you fucked in the spa or the girl you went out with for three years you were almost engaged to or that guy you only saw a couple of times and then he got back with his ex-girlfriend.

Can we not do this, Margaret?

These conversations are always about placating and consoling and assuring the other person that they have absolutely no reason to feel jealous, and then doing everything we can to ensure that they do. About dressing down and demeaning the importance of an old lover when we're feeling kindly and gentle, and then citing them as the nonpareil of lovemaking when we want to spit and spite. They're always about finally paying the piper and saying 'I've had twenty-four lovers', and Y saying 'Really. Oh . . . I've had thirty-nine', and then X quickly following up with 'But I'm not counting one-night stands. Are we counting one-night stands? Well if we're counting one-night stands then . . . three hundred and seventy-two'.

It's about summoning up some barely remembered stranger who crashed into your arms at a New Year's Eve party, a person almost completely forgotten but for our distinct memory of the remarkable smell of their genitals, and redefining him or her as an exhilarating and tempestuous partner. It's about turning the kiss into a fondle, the fondle into a grope, the grope into a head-job, the head-job into a fuck, and the fuck into an affair.

It's fucked and it's awful and it's the death of relationships and I don't want any part of it. I resolved myself a long time ago to not ever again being ensnared by the jealousy and misgivings and hurt that these figures and facts and faces can give expression to; that lie too soon beneath the surface of me; that wait and idle away the time until they can drag me weeping into despair. I am not ever going to eat my liver over this again.

I raise myself up and set my elbows on the pillow and rest my scratchy chin on my knuckles, looking to the side at the lovely woman who lies warmly beside me. She smiles at me, her eyes are pale and ghostly, and sometimes a nubilated blue and in certain lights a mardle green. She pouts out her rich lips and I press mine against hers, and then she sweetly winks her eyelashes against the tip of my nose. I close my eyes, and rest myself into this gentle, dusty massage only to be startled from it by her brutally pinching the spare flabber at the conjunction of my buttocks. 'Ha' she laughs slyly and then with delight when she sees my wince of distress and by way of revenge I give her a hardy punch on the shoulder. She punches back, and I press her arms to her side and she bites my forearms and I dig my nails into her wrists and for some moments we wrestle and bundle each other roughly over the bed, pounding each other with pillows and breaking a bout-winning clinch with a knee brought up and into the other's belly, wriggling adroitly from each other's hold and then after a moment in the cold of freedom, with our sweat chilling on our skin, wriggling as adeptly back into the other's embrace. I grab her ankle as she crawls away awkwardly like a crab, and drag her and the sheet back under me, my hardened cock resting dumbly on her leg.

She snaps herself free and climbs on top of me, her knees forcibly pinning my arms down to the mattress, and her snatch open and resting on my chest like a warm, wet kiss. Her, gnarly, winded and grinding her cunt heavily against me while I try to wrench her hand around behind her and onto my desperate, blind cock. Grunting and heaving and throwing each other around and then imperceptibly, but quite consciously, we shift into an equally strenuous tussle with each other, though with markedly different intent, still biting fiercely at each other but now with different purpose, still clasping and digging into the other's skin but now trying to pull them towards us as opposed to pushing them away. Pressing and forcing and thrusting our bodies and our sweaty and soupy organs against the other's. We break a long kiss and she lies back creamily on the pillow, her hand active under my body arched over hers, greedily tugging and fumbling with my tumescent cock.

I love this dreamy, glorious, enlaced woman and nothing will break or enthreaten that love.

— How many, William?

— Why do you ask? Why do you want to know?

— Just interested.

— Okay . . . um . . . twenty-four actually. (A slight bit of selective accounting on my part.)

— Wow. Well that's pretty neat.

— Why? What's neat?

— It's neat that we've had almost exactly the same number of lovers.

— Why? How many have you had?

— Twenty-seven including you.

THE FUCKING LITTLE SLUT!!!

Margaret

— This is a dumb party and I hate you all and the presents were all crap and you can all go home. Get out of my house. Fuck off, says William, loudly, very loudly, and to all the people gathered in their small lounge room. He throws his stubby of beer across the room and it smashes on the wall above the print of the Dürer woodcut above the mantelpiece above the small and broken gas heater. He strides off up the hallway and we hear the crash that attends him falling down and we resume talking. A few moments later he reappears.

— Sorry about that. I haven't had a party since I was seven and therefore QED I haven't thrown a tantrum at a party since I was seven so I thought what the fuck. Have you tried the punch? It's pretty cool. Someone's put vodka in it. I think. I think someone has put vodka in it. Have fun.

He lumbers up beside me (I'm standing talking to John, a guy I've brought along from work), and sheathes his hand up under the bottom and fold of my black jumper. Then with greater difficulty he hooks it back down and insinuates it in and under the elastic hem of my skirt, my pantyhose, and my knickers, until he is able to clutch my right arse cheek with his cold, wet hand.

He burbles drunkenly into my ear and I, against his wishes, try to extricate his hand from off of my butt. I say:

— William, this is John.

— Hello John. Any particular reason why you're standing in my lounge room?

— I am . . . well I'm friends with . . . well I work with . . .

— Too intriguing. John, that is just too fascinating a story. Did you hear that Margaret? John just went 'babble babble babble'. I wish we had of got it on tape. Sorry John, I'm just sort of . . . drunk I guess. How old are you?

— Thirty-six.

— Fuck. You're a grown-up. Do you want a beer?

— I'm right just at the moment. I bought some wine on the way here and . . .

— Great. Margaret, what are you trying to do?

— I'm trying to get your fucking hand off my arse.

— Can we compromise? I'll take my hand off your butt if you let me rest my lips on your nipple.

— Just get off me you fucking perve.

— Okay Okay Okay. My hand is off. The hand is off. John, I'm really interested in what you're saying. We'll have to discuss it in greater detail. Maybe at the next party. Yeah?

— Well . . . I was just . . .

— Fantastic. See . . . you're interesting on so many levels, aren't you? That's what I like about you. I'll see you later.

And he staggers off.

We're having a party. And I hope it's good.

For the last week or seven days or whatever William has sort of cooled off on me. It's not that we've had a fight or a blue or anything it's just that . . . he's seemed all fractious and niggly and we've said a lot of jaggy things.

I've asked him what's wrong and what's on his mind and whether he's happy and all and I've got a lot of 'Nothing. Why?'s' and 'Nothing really. Why?'s' and 'Yeah sure. Why?'s' and I've just not answered that imperative 'Why?'

What would I say?

'Because you seem distant. Because you seem shitty. And it all seems to be dated from that conversation we had about how many people we've fucked.'

'Cause if that's what this is all about then I'm just not having any fucking part of it.

If he's got himself uptight about that then I'm not going to help him out with it.

Was I meant to be a fucking virgin when I met him?

Was I meant to be waiting around and keeping myself fucking pure just for him?

Fuck that.

Anyway, we're having a party and I hope it's good. Well, not really 'we' but more the case that 'they' are having a party. The boys are having a party. I'm sort of part of the household and sort of not. Informally I'm allowed to have some input into house meetings but I don't think I've really got any voting rights.

As it turns out I was back at Mum and Dad's on the Thursday night when they decided to have a party, but was present on the Saturday afternoon when they did the quick 'tidy round'.

That's one thing I will always love about men. The way they tackle things. A life spent in the company of men is not complete until you've seen a group of about six or half a dozen of them address such menial tasks as moving furniture. They stand around and fold their arms and light cigarettes and measure out distances with their arms (like marionettes with one critical broken string), and they test door spaces with 'elbow-to-fingertip' measurements and then they stand around again and talk about it and pick it up for a moment, and then say 'Wait wait wait. Put it down a sec . . .' and look at it again and then conclude that the couch may as well stay where it is and if people want to dance they can fucking dance outside.

And how come they stink so much? A man puts on a singlet and he instantly smells. Is there some sort of sweat source sewn into the fabric? A man can sit in a woollen jumper and an overcoat on a beach on the hottest day of summer and he won't make a smell, but put him in a singlet and stand him next to a piece of furniture that he's considering moving and he instantly excretes an over-whelming excess of sweaty pheromones.

What amazing creatures. I love men.

So anyway; the boys are standing around and stroking their chins, leaning with greater weight on one leg or the other, folding and unfolding their arms, saying 'Geez, I don't know' and 'Do you just reckon if we . . .' and 'What we need is a . . .'

One of them—Curly I think—has gone to his room and is at work on a scale model of the couch, the lounge room, the house and the suburb.

While all this intense consideration and contemplation and deliberation goes on I and some stray little ptarmi-gan-like girl whose name I never quite caught, and who has nine earrings in her left ear and who I suspect is currently fucking Simon, go shopping at the supermarket, return and prepare about eighty little toasty things made out of corn and bacon and we marinate chicken and put chips in bowls and pour ice into the bathtub and laundry sink. The boys call us into the lounge room for a moment and show us how hard they've worked all afternoon at leaving the couch exactly where it always was, and after we've congratulated them on their industry, they go off to their respective rooms to have a little nap. In their absence What's-her-twat and I vacuum the floor and wipe down the walls and empty ashtrays and collect flowers from around the neighbourhood which we then arrange prettily in various empty beer bottles.

To pay them their due, I will commend them on the hard work they did in ensuring that their party was well attended. On Friday night each one of them made precisely one phone call to a strategically well-connected friend and said something along the lines of 'We're having a party Saturday. Tell everyone. Bye', and then returned to playing video games until sunrise.

Despite what they deserve their party is a success, and at present approximately three hundred and twenty people are scattered around the house and its garden spilling beer. I'm going a bit silly trying to retain and maintain some order, trying to control things and make sure that not too much stuff gets broken. My task is made that bit more difficult by virtue of the fact that the major misbehavers at the party are the house's occupants, who are at present stripping palings and trying to break rails from the fences and smashing up furniture to fuel an enormous bonfire they have raging in the back garden. William is absolutely pissed off his nut and is no good to anyone.

William

— What? Oh this is so cool, this is so fucked. What? Oh yeah . . . to an extent I guess. Ha. I see. Yeah I see. I see. I really can't talk about this now . . . well I can. Like yeah I can talk about it if you want to but I really fear and suspect that everything I say'll be . . . like shit.

I'm at this party and at the same time I'm at home and there's a load of fucking people here and it is too fucking scary. FUCK!! I'm out in the backyard or somewhere, I don't fucking know, I'm lost. Didn't there used to be a fence there? I'm talking to . . . fuck I don't know . . . you, I guess. Were you there? It was a fucking huge party.

Anyway, I'm talking to you. I say (probably spitting while I say it):

— How beautiful does Leanne look. I mean Margaret. How beautiful does Margaret look. I love her. I love her guts. Like . . . Wow. You probably don't believe me 'cause the way I figure it . . . you probably . . .

Fuck that.

I am so tired.

— I don't think it was even my idea to have this party. Well it was but it wasn't you know. Like I said yeah I don't mind as long as I don't have to do anything. So . . .

I want to go to bed.

— Are you right for a drink?

— There's some beer out in the laundry you can have if you want.

— I had some vodka before but someone poured it all in the punch.

— Hey, look over there . . . I mean don't look. Don't look like you're looking but when you get the chance, look over there just by the door in to the kitchen. Not now. I'll tell you when. Just make out like we're talking and all and then I'll actually . . . Now. Look now.

— Did you see the girl with the short hair? Yeah?

— That's Margaret's little sister. God I don't know like she's about fourteen or something but . . . excuse me . . . is that the world's most beautiful female or what? I have been . . . am I allowed to say 'wanking myself off silly thinking about that girl' in mixed company. No? Yeah? Probably best that I don't say that but suffice to say . . . isn't she the most elegant creature that God spat breath into.

I didn't say that.

I did not say that.

I didn't say that.

That John guy is a bit of an old sock 'ey?

Margaret

William gets more and more drunk and sweatier and sweatier and more and more red. He could do this if he was smaller. He could get drunk like this without it being an issue if he was a little person. If he looked more like an Uncle Harold or a Grandpa Wilson but as is he's too big and too threatening to let himself go like this.

He has a great capacity for kindness and a great potential for horror.

I feel him watching me from across the room. Sipping slowly from his beer and running his lips gently against the edge of the can, nodding at the pointless babble that this one or the other of his friends might be saying, all the time observing me and registering everything I do. I fall forward for a moment and spill my wine and John takes my arm and William is watching. I give John my glass and chicken wing for a moment while I fumble in my pockets for my cigarette lighter and William is watching. I repeat my telephone number to John as he keys it into his pocket-diary-organiser-computer thing and William is watching.

He is Van Blixen and Bluebeard, Nonchalance and Obsession, Indifference and Possession, Freedom and Control.

He edges up to our group; myself and this guy John, Jane and her girlfriend Rachel, and some fucking weird thing called Roy Anderson. We have been talking about the virtues and failures of the various decades. John says:

— The seventies were a dreadful decade. Everyone seemed to go to sleep for ten years.

— Oh that's brilliant, says William. I ask:

— What? What do you mean, William?

— Oh the whole seventies theory. It's just becoming a bit boring.

— Well, John is right. They were a shocking time. The music and the clothes and the television shows. Like can you believe flared trousers? I mean come on.

— What's our 'give a shit' factor on things like that, Margaret? In real terms the seventies were an amazing decade. They saw the significant consolidation of the feminist and homosexual movements, the Punk explosion, the fucking whole . . . redefinition of white-western shit, post-Watergate, Vietnam and the OPEC bloc. The formation of Bangladesh. Whitlam, Murphy, Wran. It was the most fucking shit-hot decade of the century.

— What John is probably saying . . .

— What John is probably saying is 'The book was better than the film', and 'I liked the band's early stuff, before they went commercial', and 'The seventies were a shit decade' and all those fucking trendy, shit-headed, tidy and safe crap-arsed platitudes that we can all nod to, feeling quite superior and quite smug and quite knowingly fucking cool.

John is bearing all this with admirable patience. I cannot.

— Well excuse us for all conforming to social niceties. Maybe we should all be drunk fuckwits who abuse our guests.

— Fuck you, says William and he blunders off through the crowd and away from our group.

— Sorry about all that, says John and then he nervously shifts his right foot forwards and back.

— I wasn't even born in the seventies, says Jane and she cheerily shrugs her shoulders and follows after William.

— I'm not even born now, says that mutant from hell Roy Anderson and he leans forward, blubbers and drools on Rachel's shoulder, kissing her neck and snaking his tongue into her ear, and presses his beer stubby against one of her tits. She rubs the back of her hand up and down against his cock and she smiles at me in a 'Hello sister' kind of way as if she's all grown up now and she and I are part of the same mature community.

I lean forward and whisper in her ear that she has a large stain of menstrual blood on the arse of her pretty white party dress and she runs from the room mortified.

I go out the front and cool off.

William

— Oops to an extent but fuck that.
— I agree. The guy's a jerk.

I am sitting down the back of our yard on the guinea pig cage. They scurry restlessly and frantically around their domain and I figure this is because one of the boys spent half an hour blowing dope smoke into their faces so I guess they're all stoned. The next morning will reveal that three of their company died as a result of the experience, and it is this that probably accounted for the frantic movement of the others as I sat on their cage, with Jane next to me, and one of her legs pressed gently, imperceptibly, and magnificently against one of mine. I'm thinking about whether the chicken-wire might tear and ladder her stocking. I'm thinking that maybe the wire will give way under her weight and she'll fall back and spill her drink. I'm thinking about what would happen if she fell 'splat' on Trent, Victoria or Darth.

No I'm not.

I'm thinking about that small point of contact, that slight tender kiss, that minute and breathless connection of our bodies, I'm thinking of the feel of her leg against mine. And I'm thinking about nothing else. I move my leg.

— He wasn't that bad.
— He's a fuckwit, William.

— Well I was a bit out of line.

— Fuck him. He's a loser. I just can't believe the way you can stand him creeping around Margaret the way he does.

— What do you mean?

— What do I mean? You know what I mean. The guy nearly sprogs every time he gets a look at her tits.

— 'Sprogs'?

— Cums. Blows. Shoots his wad. You know what I mean. He's a sleazy turd. You were not out of line at all.

And she rubs my leg reassuringly, and then fumbles around for a while in her small olive-green shoulder-bag. She finally claims and reveals a pouch of tobacco and a plastic lip-seal coin bag of green. From the tobacco pouch she takes two cigarette papers, runs her tongue slowly against the glue of one, and sticks them together.

— What are you doing, Jane?

— I'm um . . . playing tennis with a walrus.

— I mean . . . what . . . why have you got dope?

— Rachel got some from her brother. I'm rolling us a joint.

— I can see that. Don't you figure you're a bit young to be smoking?

— William, how old were you when you first smoked?

— Actually I was nineteen.

— Oh. Well don't you wish you had have been younger?

— I suppose so. Okay. Cool.

I take the remaining cigarette papers from her lap, where they rest on her short, black velvet skirt, tear off a bit of the cardboard, and roll up a roach.

Some forty-five minutes later and Jane and I are lying back hopelessly on the grass. During that period of time I've decided that there should be a television show where I

88

review films and comment on current affairs and occasionally turn taps on and off and prepare food, there should be a film where the trees and bushes undercut and provide a subtle comment on the actions of the human protagonists and I should review it, and that there should be another TV show about me just lying next to a guinea pig cage and talking about whatever comes into my head and how funny that would be. I've thought these thoughts and a hundred other things that won't seem at all as funny tomorrow morning, and which made no sense to Jane who has likewise made absolutely no sense to me. For the last ten minutes our conversation has generally and safely been along the lines of:

— Ha Ha. [*Outburst of laughter or guttural guffaw.*]
— What?
— Oh nothing.
— No, what?
— Really nothing.

Or words to that effect. But then Jane breaks the comfortable miasma we have settled into, and compels social skills that I'm not confident I'm capable of fulfilling.

— William . . .
— What?
— Oh . . . nothing.
— No, what?
— William . . .
— What?
— Can I tell you something?
— Sure, Jane.
— Can you promise me something?
— Anything.
— Can you promise me that you are so stoned and so drunk that you won't remember what I've told you?
— I guess. What's it about?
— Oh . . . nothing.

— No. Tell me.

— It's about Margaret and you and me.

— Me, you and Margaret?

— Yes.

— Fuck!! That's heaps of people.

— It's . . . three.

Massive laughter-break for both of us. Takes about five minutes to get over this joke.

— Um . . . what . . . what were we . . . oh cool. The me and the you and the thingo thing. What about . . . what about us, Jane?

— Oh . . . that's right. Do you promise that you won't remember this tomorrow morning?

— I promise.

— This is important. You have to swear to me that you won't remember.

— Jane, I absolutely promise.

— Well . . . I've been thinking about you and Margaret, and I've been thinking about you and me, and . . .

And I have absolutely no memory whatsoever of what she then proceeded to say.

Margaret

At least John showed some style. He helped me sober Rachel up after I'd taken her from the clutches of the Squidman Roy Anderson and then he waited with her while I went off to find Little Missy Princess Jane.

And what a sweet little couple those two made.

Cuddled up like a couple of sweet little waifs at the back of the yard.

Her, asleep and resting her pretty, little head on his manly, strong protective chest. Him—looking like the sweetest little teddy bear you ever saw—asleep but still running his stinking fingers gently through her pretty, little, tousled greasy fucking devil's hair. It only took four kicks to the head to wake him up, and his startled rising woke her, and then they blinked their sweet little koala eyes ('blinking, you know, like one not sure whether he was awake or asleep'), and stretched their pretty little bunny backs and smiled at each other shyly like two darling little snookum-pookums.

I kicked her sweet little fanny into the back of John's car, thanked him for taking my sister and her shit-blister friend home, and then went off and punched the shit out of William.

He begged, he pleaded, he apologised, he claimed innocence, he explained.

I punished him.

I relented.

The sex was fantastic. It was a berserk root, a bottle of amyl which we spilt everywhere and which chucked our brains into this wild cock-cunt hungry dance that was quite out of control. I sucked on his soul. I hate him and I hate Jane and I certainly hate myself for letting myself get this jealous. God she's my little sister, she's like ten years old or something. He loves me. This is so irrational feeling this way. There's nothing going on.

I hate her.

I hate that she can do this to me.

I hate that he can do this to me.

William

This is something that happened that annoyed the skin off me.

Margaret and I are sitting, lounging around on my bed. Midday, on a weekend. I don't know whether it's before that fucking party or after. It's around that time. During the bleak period. She's on her stomach, reading *Memories of the Ford Administration* by John Updike, her legs propped up in the air behind her like a stablecross. I'm watching her as she finishes the last page and immediately turns to discover what is revealed to be a brief bibliography (*Brief Bibliography*).

— What did you do then? I ask.

— What? When?

— Just then.

— What just then?

— Just then when you finished the book and you turned straight away to the next page.

— I don't know. I just wanted to see what came next.

— How do you mean?

— I just wanted to see if that was the end of the book.

— You're kidding.

— No. Why are you getting so hostile?

— I'm not getting hostile I just can't fucking believe that you had to turn the page to see whether that last sentence was the conclusion of the story.

— Well it probably was. Like it seemed like an end. I guess. I just turned the page to make sure.

— Give it to me. Look: 'The more I think about the Ford Administration, the more it seems I remember nothing.'

Now after what . . . 369 pages . . . doesn't that scream 'This is the fucking end' to you?

— I guess so, she says, resignedly.

Margaret

Fancy this.

I adore William, I truly do. I love the way he turns to me when his knee has been grazed or his ball is caught in the neighbour's tree or when he has lost his lunch box. And I love the way he watches me trustingly as I treat it with Mercurochrome, or beat it down with a broom, or discover it magically at the very bottom of his bag. I love the way he holds my face, and clutches my cheeks and with his thumbs tenderly rubs backwards and strokes my eyebrows as he comes inside me. I love the way he clumsily lumbers himself and his face away from mine, retreating slowly down my body, softly kissing my chin and then my neck, gently grazing his dry lips over my nipples, gingerly dusting my belly with his soft stubble, brushing a few slight, heedful kisses against my navel, and then attentively bringing his lips and tongue against my pink bits. I love the way he, with such application and intent, draws and directs and strives me towards my orgasm. And I love the way he blows stray feathers up above him, sending them floating around the room, before he dozes off to sleep, or the way he surrenders himself to the sex-sticky side of the bed, or the way he will with great deliberation herd and allocate the green and red seasoning on his barbecue shapes until there are equal majorities and minorities of both on every biscuit. I love the way he will with equal attention listen to a police officer, a child, and a turtle.

But I despair at the way he flitters and flutters his life away. He is damnable garnish.

He watches the world and all those in it with a remedial naivety; happy to swap the cow for the pretty beans, to ride on the forehead of the fox, and to sit with the wolf who calls himself a relative.

How long can this fool survive?

William

I'm losing myself. I'm losing myself in this relationship.

The other morning, I think it was morning, I was mistaken for some other fuck. I was lazing around flicking through some old copy of *Cleopolitan Fair*, learning how to appeal and hang on to a guy by losing weight and giving good head and pretending to make less money than he does according to Sharon Stone's ex-lovers and Shannen Doherty's bad behaviour, when Margaret asks me:

— Are you really going to read that again?

— Sorry wha'? I say and she just lets it go and I'm about to let it go and then I figure actually, 'What did she say?', I've never read this issue before. I've read the article. It's been reprinted a thousand times in these fucking magazines but I've never actually read this one. And I turn to her and just . . . pause. And then I said:

— Margaret, that wasn't me was it?

— No. No it wasn't. It was Dale I just got . . . sorry.

And that's cool. She's had other lovers. That's cool and fine.

But I'm losing myself. I'm losing myself in this relationship.

I'm not the one saying, 'Gee sorry. But I've just mistaken you for one of the other five million cocks I've popped. Get over it.'

Get over it, William.

Reclaim yourself.

Margaret

And this is another reservation I have about the man.

He will return in the evening from the day's hunt and with great ceremony throw down on the cooking bench a great musty sack which gives a screech of disgruntled complaint as it lands heavily on the surface. Then from within the sack he'll draw out the day's catch, eye-dazzling and brightly plumed parakeets and parrots and peacocks. Magnificent glorious birds that sit up proudly on a perch and tell wondrous stories about pirates and mermaids and redskins.

But then when we smash their heads in with a rock and rip out their guts and pluck and boil and stuff them in a pot, they shrivel and wither into small and grey pieces of stringy and unpalatable meat.

He would burn a million dollars to warm a lame donkey, scorn a thousand palaces to spend an hour on a swing, and refuse a hundred years of luxury in the belief that a minute spent with a dusty man in a dusty velvet hat, one glass eye and a tattoo of the great rivers of Canada on the palm of his hand may bring greater reward.

He is a sweet, gentle fool. And he will destroy us both.

William

There was a morning when I woke up to sound of the telephone ringing and I blindly bumbled and fumbled my hand over the bedside table and thought, 'Shit, it's not there.' Not, 'Shit, the phone's not there' but, 'Shit, the whole fucking bedside table's not there.'

When I opened my eyes and unglued the shit and pus that had sealed them closed during the night I squinted and focused and noticed that 'Shit, my whole bloody room wasn't there.'

There's a Hockney and a Dufy and a Renoir on the wall and they're not mine.

There's an open wardrobe of women's clothing and that's not mine.

There's a blind which isn't mine concealing a window that if I could see I reckon wouldn't be mine and I bet the view it revealed would not be mine, either.

Pretty much at about this point I figure I'm in someone else's room. I'm in the room of the woman I've just felt disengage herself from the bed. The woman I've just seen grab a gown and awkwardly run from the room. The woman I can hear talking on the telephone.

My head hurts, and it feels like my forehead and brain have become the focus point for all the weight and gravitational force acting upon the earth.

BOOM.

Memories start coming back, bits of dialogue and quick flashes and images.

BOOM.

— Look hi . . . um . . . it's really smoky in here and all and . . .

BOOM.

— Yeah I'm a student out at Monash Uni and I . . .

BOOM.

— I don't know. I'm kind of technically seeing a woman at the moment and . . .

BOOM.

I can see this woman talking on the phone. She's standing in a smartly decorated lounge room feigning interest in a telephone call that came way, way too early. Down on the floor beside the bed I can see a watch (it's 8.17 a.m.), a packet of Kent cigarettes, a few stray coins and a wallet. I knock the wallet open and check the driver's licence. Joanne Hillary Robertson. Joanne Hillary Robertson. The name sort of rings a bell, and it's quite a nice photograph; it's a shame she's currently wearing her morning-after face.

Joanne Hillary Robertson can see that I'm awake and she mouths a 'Hello', and she starts hamming it up a bit and putting on a little show. She rolls her eyes, a silent 'Yak, Yak, Yakkity Yak', and pretends to fire a pistol at the receiver. It's all fun and 'Gidget' kind of stuff which is fine if you're Sally Field in 1968 but not when you're Joanne Hillary Robertson at 8.17 a.m.

I pull the counterpane up over my head and rub my cold sore eyes.

— Hello.

I push the doona back and look at the sleep-battered woman who has returned to the room.

— Hi.

— Bummer about that phone call. That was my girlfriend Julie from last night. She wanted to see if I was okay.

— Cool.

— And I can't remember your name. Julie doesn't know either.

— William.

— William? That doesn't sound right.

— Richard?

— Yes. That's it. Why is it an either/or question?

— I use Richard when I'm doing something I could get in trouble for.

— I bet you don't know my name.

— I bet I do. Joanne.

Joanne's pleased. I guess she didn't want to be, she wanted to be cool and street-hardened, but in her little girl's heart she's pleased that her lover of five hours ago actually knows her name and she turns to hide her grin. I fuck up.

— I just read it on your driver's licence.

She loses the smile and her shoulders fall. I'd take back that statement if I could. I cloak the doona (blue paisley, white background) over my shoulders and stand behind her, kiss the back of her neck and nuzzle my nose in her hair. She takes the doona from my hands and holds it up, cocooning us in this sweet, warm envelope and, with my hands free, I move down her back and rub and knead her arse.

— I think it's a very pretty name.

A fuck later and I'm standing in the bathroom, running cold water through my hair and trying to get it to return to some semblance of form. My stale and crusty socks are softening to the warmth of my feet; I dressed in last night's clothes like a snake climbing back into an old skin.

Joanne Hillary Robertson has sat up in bed, pulled the doona tightly around herself, and resolved to be angry.

— Um . . . how do I get to the station?

— You'll find it.

— Okay. Sure. Um . . . do you go to the Lounge often?

— Occasionally.

— Okay . . . well . . . I'll see you later I guess . . .

So it finished like all good one-night stands, a short and terse farewell, the two players suddenly realising they were strangers, didn't know the hell about each other, and didn't like the way the other smelt. The door keys are angrily snatched from a ceramic fruitbowl on a kitchen bench, an avocado is knocked onto the floor, the keys and a lock are fumbled with and a door is closed behind me. I'm out, free, in the morning sun.

I can see the Nylex sign looming behind the buildings and the roofs so I pretty much figure I'm somewhere in Richmond and I head in the general direction of where I figure the station will be. I give it a couple of seconds just to make sure that I won't be seen, and then run my fingers quickly under my nose, like a secret agent giving a signal, the half salute that all males know. Checking for *that smell*.

I happen upon a phone booth.

— Hello, Margaret. Hi, Honey. Did I wake you? Yeah, I stayed at Paul's last night. I missed the last tram home and couldn't be bothered walking. Will I call later when you're more awake? Okay . . . see you. Bye. I love you.

Fuck You Margaret.

Suck the Pus.

I still believe in me.

You haven't got all of me yet, Girlo.

Fuck You.

Oh . . . and another thing happened recently that has kind of weirded the Dickens out of me.

It appears I flew again the other night. About a week ago.

I've done it once before (once up and up to Margaret's windowsill) and it appears I've done it again.

I could remember the night before—bits of the night before—and could remember the feel of the wind as it beat against me, lifting my arms up and away from my body, the fast food wrappers and cans and bottles that bounced and bulleted past me, surrendering themselves to the wind's force. I can remember feeling myself gradually lifted, slowly at first, and then more markedly, about an inch off the ground, my feet bumping dumbly against the footpath and flailing up madly, and then finally I was off—and up—and sweeping high above the streets, watching the cars and the people and the lights and the houses and the souls and the lives idling below.

And the odd dog.

As the wind rolled and tossed and tumbled me through the dark heavens and then elected to dump me high up in some fucking tree.

Weird.

I woke up to the sound of the morning birds (correction: the very fucking early morning birds. The birds that wake up the morning birds.) high up in a tree (too high to have climbed), and had I woken with a start I would have fallen a great distance and landed with a crash on what looked like a sprinkler attachment, a large stick, and an ankle.

And a cat called Missy Missy Missy.

I was surrounded by foliage, in a tree in Mount Waverley, nestled close to Jane's window, and damned uncomfortable.

I don't know what the hell I was doing there but it was considerably spooky.

I watched Jane wake up.

Watched her stretch and arch her back, sweetly rub the sleep from her eyes.

Watched her fold back the covers and iron them across her breasts gently with the palms of her hands.

Then I fell from the tree—a considerable distance—and landed with a crash on a stick, my left ankle and what was in fact a casting model of a crankshaft from a V8 engine.

Not—in fact—a sprinkler attachment.

Missy Missy Missy was momentarily startled by my sudden appearance, but she quickly regrouped and rebuilt and confirmed her acceptance of the situation by licking me gingerly on the nose

It tickled.

I'm not sure what this whole flying thing means but it spooks me.

It all seems rather irregular.

Sure . . . I'm glad I can fly, it makes me feel rather special though I'm not sure I can find any great use for it.

In fact I foresee circumstances in which having the gift of flight may be inopportune or at least slightly embarrassing.

Margaret

This is a conversation I have with William at about this time.

We are sitting around on a Friday night, it's early, it's about ten, and we haven't yet made our plans for the evening. William is with great attention scouring his pubic hairs for pubic crabs, a particular type of irritating creature that has recently made home upon both of us, and which has proliferated in an alarming fashion. Neither of us has with any great intent taken the other to task for their appearance, and if I had thought about this at the time, I probably would have realised that this was a silent affirmation of the other's infidelity. Instead, I just scratched. William, though, is scraping them from his skin with a match-stick which he then uses to crush them, each time smiling with satisfaction when he hears the distinctive 'crack' sound they make when squashed. He is happy and contented and at peace, and looks like some bastard-mutant Gorilla in the Mist. It seems he would be content to do this for hours; brushing the pubic hair back, holding his cock and balls out of the way, seizing on any blotch or discolouration with vigour, scraping at it eagerly, and seemingly disappointed when it reveals itself to be only a freckle or dermatological blemish. Happy when he finds a true crab, perhaps down on the hairs at the base of his scrotum, so that he can draw it up and skin it from the pube with a pair of tweezers, then study it with scientific interest as it wriggles and waves its limbs around as he sets it on the ledge, and before he brings down the match upon it.

CRACK!!

Brush, brush, scrape, scrape, squeeze . . . squeeze . . . silence.

CRACK!!

His entertainment is brought to a premature termination by the very success of his industry, the last five minutes of searching his pubes frantically has not been rewarded with any stray discoveries and he looks up at me disappointedly, eyes my bush yearningly and then collects his equipment (the tweezers, the matches), and starts lumbering over the bed towards my cunt. I swing my legs around and sit up on the bed, put a pillow over my lap, and say:

— William . . .

— What? he says, looking sadly at my new position, and then fiddling absentmindedly with the tweezers and matches.

— William . . . what do you want out of life?

— What do I want out of life?

— Yes. What are your ambitions?

— Ambitions?

— Yes. What do you want to achieve in life?

— In my life?

— Yes.

— God, what a weird question. This sounds like an Amway spiel. Are you about to try to sell me Amway?

— No, William.

— Or Jesus. Are you about to sell me Jesus?

— Will you answer the question?

— What was the question?

— Oh you're just fucked.

— Well shit, Margaret. I don't know. You know . . . I don't think I've ever really thought about it.

— Well think about it now, William.

— Okay. Let me see . . . No. Nothing. Drawn a blank. Can't think of a thing. Why?

He scratches thoughtfully at his pubes, scratches the underside of his cock, and then gives it a couple of rough hard yanks.

— Well, come on. Try harder. What would make you happy?

— You make me happy, Margaret.

— No. I'm not asking you because I want to hear you say that. I'm just . . . I want to know what you're about. Who you are. What would make you happy?

— Okay . . . Okay Okay. I've got it. What would make me happy? I guess . . . you know . . . enough money to be able to buy a six pack of beer and a packet of cigarettes each day.

Pause.

— Are you serious?

— I guess so. Yeah . . . that'd be good.

— Is that all you need, William? Cigarettes and a half dozen?

— Okay . . . eight. Eight cans of beer.

— And that's it?

— Well maybe a slab on weekends.

— What about owning a house?

— Oh yeah . . . that'd be nice, I suppose.

— Or a car?

— A car would be great!! Toot Toot. I could go Toot Toot.

— And what about children?

— Kids?

— Yes kids, William.

— It depends.

— On?

— Depends on how much of my beer they'd drink.

105

— WILL YOU BE FUCKING SERIOUS FOR ONCE IN YOUR FUCKING LIFE!!

— Okay Okay. Chill, all right Margaret. Yes . . . I'd like to have children one day.

— Well . . . more children than you've got already.

— Ha Ha. Touché. Up yours, Margaret. I mean I'd like to have . . . a . . . 'family' one day. Children I was allowed to see. Yes, that'd be really lovely.

— Well . . .

— Well what?

— Well, how do you think you are going to get any one of those things if you just wank away in part-time jobs all your fucking life?

— I don't know. Shit. Something will work out. It always does.

— So that's it?

— What? What's it?

— That's your whole approach to life? Something'll fucking work out?

— I guess . . . you know . . . my parents'll die and I'll get all their money.

— You're just fucked in the head, William.

He looks away sadly for a moment, and then scratches vigorously at his arse. He pauses, frowns slightly, rummages around in the pubes that frame his little pink rectum, and then slowly brings out, and around, his thumb and forefinger which are pressed together tightly. He stares at them intently, slowly draws them apart, careful not to drop the parasitic treasure that they do in fact ultimately reveal, and which he sets on the ledge and then abandons as he searches for a match.

CRACK!!

— Margaret . . .

— What!!

— Why am I fucked again? I never really figured . . .
why . . . exactly.

William

We love the way Jane Scarborough takes a head job.

She's a bit mixed up and reckless but she's dropped all
the rough crap from the deal.

A nice delicate root.

We just love lying back, her, sitting up above us, her
cunt just out of reach, waiting and lingering and kind of
unsure.

It's like trying to feed a deer, a dear sweet little fawn,
and slowly, tenderly coaxing it forward. Carefully, gingerly,
coyly and then . . . a light brush of soft, wet-wet, flesh
nubs mindfully against our face; brushes, drifts slightly
against our unshaven chin and leaves a light smear of
blush damp on our skin. Then I'll lose it, I'll just get too
enamoured by the sexual delicate balance of it all and
grasp her by the arse and force and bring her down onto
my face and lap at her wet lips and she'll move back . . .
I blew it . . . and again we play this gentle coax-and-tempt
game.

Again she settles down onto me and again she with-
draws access when I get too forceful . . . when I deliver
myself up to myself.

I love this timid jittery-cunt thing that some women
have got going.

Margaret?

Well if you go in for getting clobbered around the face,
and dutch-rubbed and smothered with a cold, stinking,
wet clot of clammy flesh then she's probably just the ticket.

Margaret

And this conversation happens a couple of days later.

We are lying back on his bed in a state of comparative post-sexual bliss. The sex was a slightly irregular and novel sensation by virtue of the fact that the day previously William had carefully trimmed and then eventually shaved all the hair from around his organs. On any other person this would probably have solved the pubic crab problem, but as William is so amply adorned with body hair it was a fairly simple task for the crabs to uproot themselves and disperse. To abandon their traditional home when life there became too disruptive and migrate to other pastures, to the moist and sweaty hairs behind his knees, to his underarms and to his lower legs, and to the wide and hairy field of promise that is his back. I'm not too sure how disappointed or concerned William is with this diaspora of the pubic crabs to whom he plays host, it seems to have only enlarged the hunting grounds where they can be isolated and accounted for, and hence to have enlarged his opportunities for play. William says he feels sorry for the crabs; that to be a creature that makes its home in the pubic hair of another creature must be the most fucked existence on earth. He qualifies this by saying that it mightn't be so bad if they were the pubic hairs of Winona Ryder and in those circumstances he would probably be quite happy to be a crab. Her, or Mary Stuart Masterson. Or Liz Phair. Or a young Katherine Hepburn. After a few moments pause he tactfully adds my name to the list of women whose pubic hairs he would happily inhabit as a crab.

Am I meant to thank him for that?
Jesus!!

— Hey, Margaret . . .
— Hey what?
— Is that one there? Just where I'm pointing on my shoulder. Can you see one there?
— Fuck Off.

— Hey, Margaret . . .
— What!!
— I was thinking about what you said the other day about my life and all and about how I'm sort of wasting away and you know . . .
— Yes.
— And I figured . . . well I think you had a bit of a point there.
— And?
— And I've done something about it.
— Really . . . ?
— Yeah. Yeah. 'I've taken con-trol of my destiny.'
— So what have you done?
— Well I'm going to resign from my job at the bookshop . . .
— You are kidding!
— Yeah . . . and I'm going to be a full-time writer.
— What!?!
— Yeah, I'm just going to write. Like . . . full time. Novels and books and plays and stuff. It'll be cool.
— What are you going to do for money?
— Well, I'll go on the dole.
— William, are you serious?
— Well at least I'm the only one out of all of our friends who's staying true to the cause.

— William, what particular cause is it that requires that you spend your whole life lying around and getting pissed and stoned?

— Look, I don't know. Socialism or something, I don't know how it works. I thought this was what you wanted. You were the one who said I had to think about what I was doing with my life.

— You really don't get it, do you, William?

— Get what?

— Get how fucked in the head you are.

— Hey, Margaret . . .

— What?

— Oh . . . nothing.

— No. What do you want now?

— Can I borrow fifty bucks until Thursday?

— Fuck off.

William

Jane Palmer came into the bookshop the other day. Like I'm just standing there and all of a sudden she's there. Her heavy bag full of school things hefted up on her shoulder, the blazer laced through the handles and resting on the top, the one hip jutting out and assisting to take the weight of the heavy bag, making her look for all the world like a very sweet ampersand (&).

She is very sweet is our Jane.

She had in her company one particularly unattractive young school friend, a fat and pimply girl with dull greasy hair that hung down and stuck to her cheeks. What is it about pretty girls and ugly girls? How is it that they seek each other out and bond with each other? It's something like how in Africa you always see the zebras chumming around with the bullocks because the bullock can't see well but it can hear for great distances and the zebra can't hear but it's got good eyesight, or maybe vice-versa, but whatever the facts the thing is they form an unlikely but inseparable pair. It's like they've figured that a good thing equals two average and pretty girls ($X = Y + Y$), but at the same time and similarly you can achieve that same correct equation through: $X = Y - Z + Y + Z$.

Is that right?

I think that's right. Can you tell I've started hanging around with a friend who knows a bit of maths?

Jane is very pretty.

And she came into the bookshop.

Reason?

No real reason.

She said she came to visit me.

And to buy a copy of *Lolita*.

!?!

Margaret

Beer is not food.

Beer is not in, of or by its very essence food.

Beer is nice to drink before food.

Beer is a good thing to drink while eating food.

And beer is sometimes a nice thing to drink after consuming food.

But beer is not food.

Food is food.

How can I impress upon William that you cannot go for five days consuming nothing but beer.

It's just ridiculous.

I need to eat.

I need food.

Sorry, but as a member of the human race I need something solid that I can chew.

And if I hear him one more time suggest that I could put ice in my beer I will kick his stupid, ugly, gorgeous goddamned face in down to the skull.

William

Margaret and I are definitely going to finish up together.

I kind of hoped and prayed and thought we one day would, but I kind of wasn't sure, considering the way things have been going lately . . .

Jesus, the way things have been going lately.

But now it is certain.

We will finish up together and get married and have a family and all.

There is now indisputable proof.

It is written.

Margaret

Curly is one day going to get married and live in Florence with three children.

One of the twins is going to be a fireman and will probably one day learn how to juggle.

The other twin is quite likely to one day find the light sabre that he lost from his Obi Wan Kenobi action figurine over fifteen years ago, will never have a cannibalistic experience either as eatee or eater, but is definitely going to marry one of the Kennedy nieces.

And apparently William and I are going to get married.

How do I know these things?

Because for the last fucking five nights William and the boys have sat huddled around the fucking coffee table and put a pubic crab in the middle of four rectangles drawn on a piece of paper. Each rectangle contains a wish or likely future that each boy has devised for himself: 'Will I ever . . .' or 'Who will I . . .' Then they watch spellbound to see into which rectangle the crab eventually crawls.

William is the big high priest of this insidious order of deranged fucks, and will return with great ceremony from his room whenever a new crab is required; they all die eventually, either from exhaustion or murder, when one of the boys is unhappy with the prophecy the crab intuits.

Now it's not just me, is it?

This is fucking weird, sick, deranged, creepy behaviour.

Nibs may or may not one day have a pet lamb called George and he may or may not yet become a pirate. (Someone bumped the table.)

Fuck!!

William

These are some telephone calls I receive, and a conversation I play some small role in, over the next couple of weeks.

Phone Call # 01.

RING, RING. BREEP, BREEP. TINGLE, TINGLE. (Or whatever.)

— Yes, hello.
— Hello. William?
— Is that Jane?
— Hi. Is my sister there?
— No she's not. What's wrong?
— Nothing's wrong. I just wanted to know whether she's got Dad anything for his birthday yet.
— You're kidding.
— No. Why?
— Well hell, Jane. It's late. She's around at Georgia's. You knew that. Don't ring her there, it's . . . what is it . . . it's three in the morning.
— I can't sleep.
— Put one of your pillows under your feet.
— What?
— It'll work. Just try it. Goodnight.
— What were you doing?
— I was asleep. Goodnight Jane.
— Were you dreaming?
— No . . . I don't know . . . yes, yes I was.
— What was it about?

— I was driving my parents out to Tullamarine Airport.
— Where?
— To the airport.
— Are they going on a big long trip?
— Yes. No. I don't know it's not even them anyway.
— Why?
— 'Cause sometime while we're on the freeway it turns out that they're not my parents. They're actually my grade three teacher Miss Hetherington and the guy who plays the little, mad guy in 'Hill Street Blues' and when we get to the airport it's actually the Taj Mahal.
— Oh.
— Pretty dull, I guess. Can I go now? By the time I get back to sleep and we get their shit through luggage and all you know.
— Goodnight William.
— Goodnight Jane. Try the pillow thing.

Phone Call # 02.

BREEP, BREEP. BREEP, BREEP.

I stumble, and blunder, and flounder about with the phone.

— Yes, hello.
— Hi William.
— What is it Jane?
— Is Margaret there?
— Yes. Do you want to talk to her?
— No.
— What do you want at this hour?
— Do you know what a cootie is?
— No. But I'm sure that if you go to school tomorrow you'll find one in Burris Ewell's hair.
— How did you know I was reading *To Kill a Mockingbird*?

— Because you know the word cootie, and you're in Year 9, and everyone reads it.

— Did you like it?

— It's one of the most perfect books ever written. It's a shame everyone gets the shits with it because they have to read it for school.

— I'm liking it.

— You're only up to page 32.

— Well it's good so far.

— Is that all Jane?

— Do you think Atticus is giving it to Calpurnia?

— Goodnight Jane.

— Wait a second.

— What?

— Oh . . . nothing . . . nothing really . . . Goodnight William.

— Goodnight Jane.

— Was that my sister? mumbles Margaret, who is drowsy, half awake, but roused into action, and she smears a trail of salty sweat on my shoulder as she leans over me to get some water from the plastic orange and mango juice bottle that sits on the table by my side of the bed. She sits up and drinks from it, spilling a good percentage down her front and onto her pale, blubbery, sheet-creased breasts and gulping noisily. I can smell her stale BO emanating from the small daub she left on my shoulder, sodden and cold, and I rub at it furiously with my hand.

— Yes. It was.

— What the fuck did she want?

— She wanted to know whether I thought Atticus Finch and Calpurnia were having sex.

— Oh. I never read that into it. What do you think?

— Maybe. A couple of times when the kids were young.

— You really think so?

— No.

— Has Jane got a mega-crush on you or what?

— Don't be stupid.

— She's got a photo of you on her folder.

— She's got a photo of everyone on her folder.

— Not one of me.

— Well as if she would.

— How many of your other girlfriends' little sisters rang you up and asked you whether fictional characters were fucking?

— Most of them. Usually about Sam Gamgee and Frodo Baggins.

— Who?

— And Gollum . . . hence his raunchy *nom de guerre*.

— What are you on about?

— Nothing. It's a *Lord of the Rings* joke. It doesn't matter.

— Oh. Haven't read it.

— You really haven't read it?

— No. Is it good?

— No, it's a crock of shit, but you still should have read it.

— Oh, she says.

She is a bit more alert and awake now, moving around restlessly and dragging the doona from off my shoulders, and hugging my hot water bottle to her stomach. Holding it against her flabby, fat, round, pale, maggoty, pox-ridden, criminally-ugly belly. Stinker Belly. Belly of Satan. The Devil's belly. She leans over and tugs on my cock for a few minutes and then we have a quick fuck. I don't even bother following up the orgasm that for a few moments seems likely to occur, though Margaret seems to enjoy her couple. We lie back in a post-sex, post-everything bliss-shit-thing, or at least feign its qualities, and then she asks:

— What do you think of her?

— Who?

— Jane.

— She's okay.

— Okay?

— Yeah . . . she seems okay.

— And that's it?

— She's a good kid.

— Nothing else?

— She's got a lot of confidence.

— That's it?

— Yes.

— Really?

— Well. No actually, Margaret. She can be a real rude little bitch. I can't believe how rude she is to me sometimes.

— You certainly seemed pretty cosy together at your party.

— I've already explained that . . .

— Yeah, yeah. You've explained.

— I've told you we spent the whole time bitching with each other.

— You were cuddling up to each other like you'd been lovers for thirty years.

— We were stoned.

— And that's the other thing. I can't believe you gave her dope.

— Well actually . . . no. It doesn't matter.

— No, William. It really doesn't matter.

— Look. She's a smart-arse little bitch. She's been rude to me from day one. She's stirring me all the time. She's just a rude little girl.

— Well . . . that doesn't matter really, does it?

— Gee thanks for the back-up, Margaret. What do you mean it doesn't matter?

— Well . . . it's just not relevant.

— Not relevant?

— Not relevant with her.

— What the fuck do you mean?

— Well . . . don't you notice anything else about her?

— No.

— Anything different?

— What are you on about, Margaret? Your little sister is just a rotten, spoilt little bitch. That's all.

— Something strange?

— What, is she sick or abnormal or something?

— No . . . well in a way.

Margaret pauses, as if she is summoning up and collating half-considered thoughts and barely resolved ideas.

No actually, that's not quite true. She pauses like someone who is [*summoning up and collating half-considered thoughts and barely resolved ideas*]. There is something slightly stagey at this moment. Margaret is performing as someone who apparently is only thinking the ideas through as they speak them. These thoughts have been considered and the conclusions drawn long before Margaret found herself in a bed with some guy and felt compelled to wipe her stinking sweat all over him. I'm really unnecessary here. This isn't a William–Margaret based thing it's a monologue that she's scripted and worked out years ago and now has to voice in the company of a second person, and by circumstance that person is me. This is a fucking act.

— William . . .

And so what? Now I'm meant to say 'What?' and she'll say 'Oh nothing', and then I'll say 'No, really, tell me. What are you thinking, darling?' and all this shit and I'll be Abbott to her Costello or Isabel to her Burton or Patroclus to her Thersites, and feed her the lines and build up her cues and focus her spotlight. Well fuck that. I'm not going to be a part of this shit. I say:

— Do you want to go to the footy tomorrow?

She pauses. Slightly cast from her intent, but after a moment taking stock she forges on:

— You're changing the subject. William . . .

But I can forge as well. I do good forge. I forge on at my own intent. I ask:

— Do you like green? I like green.

Margaret doesn't know what's going on at all. She is watching me intently, studying me with her shitty little beady eyes, looking for the crinkle in the corner of my mouth that reveals my humour that reveals the joke, or the rustle of my skin or the discolouration of my neck that will show that we're both in on the joke. I ignore her. Watch me. Study me. Do what you fucking like, I am never going to say, 'What?'

— William. I'm trying to work something out here I'm trying to . . .

— ('What?') It's kind of like this fourth colour that's just there knocking on the door but never quite makes it. It's like . . . you think about colours and you think blue, red, yellow, green. And then you think, 'Who the fuck are you green? You're just yellow and blue. Piss off back to the little league with purple and . . . orange.' But it is up on those colours. It's a major colour and yet it's kind of not. Weird.

After due pause:

— Maybe I'm wasting my time, William. Maybe you wouldn't understand . . .

Oh, good tactic. She's turning this around on to me. She's making the failing mine. Bullshit. If you want to say something, say it. Don't fucking prod me into prodding you into saying it. Margaret is very good at this bullshit-relationship stuff. So now I'm meant to say 'I'm sorry, darling. What were you thinking?'

She's good. I'm better. 'Cause I'm a cunt.

— It's like rectangles. You think square, circle, triangle, rectangle. And then you think 'Hey rectangle. You fucking top quality shape wanna-be. Piss off.' Who does rectangle think he is? Or the Mummy. You know you think Dracula, Frankenstein's Monster and the Wolfman. And then there's the Mummy. Epstein. He's another one. How the fuck did that guy become a sweathog? Always the quintessential number four. Knocking at being a member of the big three but never quite making it. That's why I like green.

Margaret bites the bullet:

— Is Jane not the most remarkably beautiful-looking person you've ever seen?

— What? (Fuck. Damn.)

— She's beautiful, William. Really beautiful.

— Oh Christ. Yes I guess so. She's kind of cute. (I can't believe I said 'What?')

— Kind of cute?

— I suppose she's quite pretty. (I want that 'what' back.)

— You suppose?

— Look I don't know what you want me to say, Margaret. Your sister is a stuck-up little brat.

— But she's beautiful. She's the most beautiful creature on earth.

— Well she needs to learn some manners.

— No. I don't think so. People like her are sort of above manners.

— Oh you're fucking weird.

— No I'm not. I guess it's just different for me because . . . you know . . . I guess it's like being Jesus's little brother or something. Or like . . . Frieda Minogue. The unsung third sister. Life's a bit strange when your little sister is a goddess.

— I really hadn't noticed.

— Of course you'd noticed, William. It's sweet of you to say that but of course you'd noticed. She's glorious.

— Well, as I figure it, I think I've chosen the right Palmer girl for me, I say, and then fatso, stinking bitch next to me says:

— Mmm . . . that's nice, and she leans up and kisses me, breathing into my face the most pungent, rancid, sleep-crusted, garlic-foul breath, breath that would wither fruit, breath that would peel paint, breath that would tarnish bronze, breath that would shame a shit-eater, the most putrid breath that I have ever inhaled in my life.

I almost vomit.

Phone Call # 03.

RING, RING. RING, RING.

— Yes, hello.

— Is she there?

— No, Jane.

— What are you doing?

— I was building a space castle.

— What?

— What do you think I was doing? I was asleep.

— Were you dreaming?

— Yes. I'm still trying to get Miss Hetherington and what's-his-head through customs.

— Still that dream?

— No. No. I wasn't dreaming. What do you want?

— Do you dream often?

— No. Not often.

— Do you have many wet dreams?

— Goodnight Jane.

— Really . . . I have to know. It's for religious studies.

— As if you have to know whether your older sister's boyfriend has wet dreams for religious studies.

— Well I've got to know about the male body. We're doing sex ed.

— You do sex ed in Religious Studies?

— Well it's not really Maths or English or anything.

— God you Catholics are weird.

— Answer my question.

— Goodnight Jane.

— Well do you?

— Jane, goodnight.

— Just tell me.

— I'm not going to talk about stuff like that with you.

— Well just tell me whether you do.

— Jane!!

— Tell me.

— Kind of . . .

— What?

— Yes. Yes I do. Not often. Not like as often as when I was young.

— Why not?

— Just because.

— Why not?

— 'Cause I don't think the sperm is building up as much. I'm sort of . . . coming more often.

— Do you masturbate, William?

— What?

— I can ask that. Do you still masturbate? It's just like a . . . *Cleo–Cosmo* question.

— Go to sleep, Jane.

— Do you?

— No. Yes. Occasionally. Sometimes.

— What do you think about?

— When?

— When you're pulling yourself off.

— Trees.

— Trees?

— Igloos.

— Igloos?

— Dinosaurs.

— Dinosaurs?

— Dinosaurs in Nazi uniforms.

— Do you think about Margaret?

— I think about stegosauruses.

— How long does it take you?

— Go to sleep, Jane.

— How long?

— This is a really 'eek' conversation.

— How long?

— Four minutes.

— Four minutes?

— About four to eight minutes.

— Is that all?

— Go to sleep. Don't ring me anymore Jane. Don't ring me again.

— Why not?

— Because I'm only polite to you because you're my girlfriend's little sister.

There's silence from the other end of the telephone and then she says quietly:

— I'm going.

— I didn't mean that, Jane. I like you. I think you're lovely. Just . . . let's not have these types of conversations. Goodnight Jane.

— Goodnight William.

I don't really masturbate thinking about dinosaurs.

I masturbate thinking about Jane.

A lot.

Margaret

William is moving away from me. He's breaking camp, bumping out, throwing in the towel.

It's nothing said, or stated, between us. We're not fighting (My God I wish we were), and it's nothing tumultuous or passionate (Jesus I wish it was).

It's just a quiet lack of interest in each other.

We can't . . . we can't break out of it now. We're amazingly polite, and amazingly loving to each other . . . but it's because of the death of passion.

If he told me that he hated me I'd know that he still loved me.

If he screamed at me that he wished I were dead I'd know that he still couldn't live without me.

If he swore at me that he despised me and could kill me and that I nauseated him then I'd know that he loved me, and cherished me, and adored me with all his heart and all his soul.

But instead we congratulate each other on our appearance, wish each other well and good health, listen with interest and attention to the other's tales and fables, and fuck with love and consideration and concern.

This is sick.

You'll lose me, you deranged bastard.

Love me.

Claim me.

Screech at me.

Damn me to hell.

I love you, William.

Make my life anguish.

John called the other night.

III

'Not so much as a sorry-to-lose-you between them.'

<u>Peter Pan</u>
J.M. Barrie

Aunt Peggy left Launceston and went to Melbourne where she worked hard and alone in the laundry of the great convent, the sweat pouring down her brow and running in torrents down her neck, the steam rising from the coppers and hueing her arms and forehead a flush, hot pink. Then she'd leave late at night, wander out into that same cold and chillsome darkness that had seen her to work in the morning; that had made her shiver and draw her hands up into the hem of her thin jumper, the dark that had escorted her to the door of the laundry, and then had idled away the day; kicking a can in the alley with some children, dozing off in the park and being pecked at by a haughty duck or so, wandering the streets and looking in the shop windows, until such moment as it was time to meet the young and lonely and lovely girl at the wash-house. He is her only companion. He is waiting when she pushes open the heavy door from the laundry, a moment's hope flits across her face until she sees him, sees the dark and another night. And then he walks her home, lets her carry him on her shoulders 'ntil she staggers and falls under his weight. She treads lightly up the long stairwell to her room, having too often been cursed and abused and scratched and spat upon by the other tenants of the guest house, and at the second landing she falls and crinks her ankle when the baby and disease so wrench her inside as they set about killing their mother and home. And then she goes to bed and lies under the few thin blankets; and worries about her sad little sister with the missing teeth, might smile warmly at the memory of Boy with his schemes and stratagems, and will treasure and remember and recite in her

129

mind the few and infrequent words her father ever said to her. Remember with pride the day she came shyly down the stairs in the new hat and he looked up from the shoes he was polishing on brown paper at the kitchen table and said, 'You look beautiful, Peg.'

She might arch her back and put her hands to the base of her spine and then smile demurely when she remembers what it felt like to have the boy hold her in his arms, what it was like to feel his weight and heavy body press on hers, and remember how she noticed how very musty and clammy he had felt. And remember how sweet his tobacco breath smelt, and how he cupped her cheeks in his gentle and rough hands, and how alarmed and frightened and joyous and bewildered he looked just when he was about finishing with his business and what he was doing.

Aunt Peggy left Neverland to have the secret baby and to catch the bubonic plague and she died a week after giving birth to her baby and she died in the Exhibition Buildings which had been converted to a hospital; or a warehouse for people who are dying of the bubonic plague. She never held that dear baby or fed it her milk or put Mercurochrome on its grazed knees or elbows or held it up to the sun shining through an unwashed window.

At that time they wouldn't let people go to the North Island from Tasmania; so as the plague could if possible be restricted to the Mainland, and so Aunt Peggy died without family, but rather died alone.

She died alone; alone in a big, dark room surrounded by a couple of hundred people.

Not that anyone knew.

My great grandmother got a departmental letter saying your daughter is dead and your grand-daughter is alive but mentally retarded due to the mother's illness during the pregnancy. And then she went to Melbourne and after due time returned with the baby and Aunt Sis, who'd been working in Ballarat, and most people thought the baby was my great grandmother's, except for Billy Wakefield who had been courting Aunt Sis, and he thought the baby

130

was hers and he left her and married a girl whose father owned the bakery on Wellington Street.

And John said to Nana Welsh, 'There was no reason for Peggy to die.'

He would have married her.

If she only had have told him.

'I would have married her. If only she had of told me.'

He would have married her and she wouldn't have left Tasmania and she wouldn't have caught the plague in Melbourne and she wouldn't have died and Boo wouldn't have been born and lived retarded, and she should have told him.

But instead a young and brave girl left her home and went to die in Melbourne at the age of nineteen.

And this was all a long time ago.

So long ago.

She would have been ninety-five this year if she had have lived.

And I never knew her.

I don't know this wonderful girl.

I never heard her cries of pain in birth and in death.

I never saw her laughter as she pushed my grandmother down the big hill near their farm in the unnamed town.

I never saw her draw breath, with fear and excitement, as she left the boat that had brought her to Melbourne.

I don't know this girl.

But the reason we're sitting here and addressing this is because I think it's goddamned awful that my frightened, silly, tragic, brave, lonely, beautiful Aunt Peggy died alone in a big and sullen room; too small to fight the death that overwhelmed her, too weak to resist the cold that rose and overtook her.

I think that's the fucking pits.

There are two types of people in the world that ne'er grow up. There are the boys who never grow up. They are the men who crowd the spare rooms or rumpus rooms of the million houses with train-sets or billiard-tables or intricate models of sailing ships and aeroplanes and dune-buggies, who leave the accounts and the gas bills for their wives to take care of, and who wax the cars and stoke the barbecues and eagerly engage their eldest daughter's new boyfriends in conversation. While the ladies do this or that these child-men will slowly and at great length explain the intricacies and benefits of this new power drill or fishing reel or camera or book, while new boyfriend #01 stands politely silent, fiddling with a stray coin of no certain denomination that he has found in his pocket, and wills his girlfriend's return.

And there are the girls who never grow up. They are the ones who die. They lie in tragic rows in our graveyards, with the humble markers and date tags, (Peggy Welsh 1902–1920) that make the soul and heart despair.

Aunt Peggy was marked to die when she dreamed of flying from the Mainland to Neverland. She died because a stupid, wilful society deemed it incorrect that a young woman fly and swoop and cavort with faeries and Indians and pirates, that she sit and hear the mermaids singing, that she have sex before marriage.

She died because she loved.

She died because she was.

Poor girl.

William

So get this. This happened.

This actually happened.

This happened recently.

Now . . . Margaret and I are going through a . . . patch at the moment.

I agree and concede that.

We've both been holding back, skirting and circling and . . . gauging the other, waiting for the other to make the move that we're holding back ourselves. Challenging the other one to . . . broach.

Sitting out the hateful silence.

Waiting for something to happen.

And then this happened.

I'm in a taxi. I've been around at Margaret's. I don't know and don't give a shit where the hell her parents have been.

Out.

And we've been just kind of like . . . you know, sitting around and we've had a pizza and all and then after a while she says like she's tired and wants to get an early night and I'm not welcome to . . . you know, I can't stay the night, I can't crash over, so twenty minutes later I'm in a taxi to come back home.

That's okay.

That's fine.

That's the way it goes around and comes back up.

That's okay. I wish you had have said 'Hey William. There's something I've wanted to . . .' but you didn't so that's cool and maybe next time or . . .

After a while the taxi driver . . . He turns around and says to me:

— There been a party there?

And I say:

— No. Just . . . Why?

And the taxi driver says:

— Oh. I just heard a call over the radio for another pick-up from that address. That's all.

So I'm sitting there, right, I'm sitting there and . . . this is a girl I've gone out with for Jesus alone knows how long for now and . . . she doesn't want to watch a video or anything 'cause she's sleepy-bubs, so I do the right thing and I leave in a taxi and there's no stress and then ten minutes later it's 'voom' . . . she's up and off and out somewhere.

So I get the taxi driver to do a U-turn and we're back in her street and it's dark and all and it's pitch black and I don't know . . . maybe there's a light breeze rustling through the trees and maybe somewhere some dad looks up from his newspaper or a baby cries or a forest moves or a bird eats its own young I don't know 'cause all I can hear is my heart going 'BOOM BOOM BOOM'.

And then this other taxi looms up from behind us, she runs out and gets in the cab and I can see the back of her head from the interior light of the taxi and we follow her, looming after her, like a remora following its brooding patron and master through the chilly waters of the night. We race through traffic lights and thunder across railway tracks, the hunted and the hunter. At one stage we pull up beside her at an intersection and I duck, hide, stretched out, furious, shuddering against the vinyl seat.

She lights a cigarette and for a moment her face is illuminated in profile and her features are sharp and drawn.

In this way we raced through the night, nearing town, nearing some rendezvous, nearing some assignation, two glowing pods threading their way through the dark, racing to an answer and hurtling towards their destiny.

Then I got the driver to stop off at a bottleshop to get some beers and we never quite found them again after that.

I got the driver to take me to a pub and I got spastic.

Then we had the next day.

Margaret

It's a Grand Final barbecue.

A Grand Final barbecue performed as only tertiary students can do; with all the trappings and accoutrements of your generic, clichéd Australian middle-class barbecue affair, with the aprons and implements and characters that we have witnessed attend such affairs as hosted by our parents and their friends throughout our childhood, but conducted with a deliberate mocking.

Overplayed with the whisper of a smile.

The boys make battle for supremacy at the hotplate, the females overzealously congratulate each other on the crispness of their salads and the prettiness of their frocks.

We natter and chatter and giggle, quietly amused by ourselves, while the boys roar and cheer at the opening ceremony of the big game; congratulating the various adolescent dancing girls prancing around the arena in their sparkly cunt-cutter leotards, congratulating them on the splendour of their appearance and the perkiness of their little titty-buds with lusty and horny acclaim and platitudes that come a bit too readily to their lips.

William likes football.

Cheers.

Football is likeable.

William says that Australian Rules Football is the most democratic of all sporting codes, the most unprejudiced and undiscriminatory.

He says that it doesn't matter whether a player is tall, short, stocky and solid, slow, lithe or fleet-footed, they all have equal opportunity to find a position and be a champion at the game.

He says that it is the most egalitarian game in the history of sport and competition.

He says this without noting or thinking for a moment that in the one hundred years that Australian Rules Football has been played there has not been a single female who has played the game professionally.

This Grand Final day doesn't look like it's going to be too pleasant.

It's cloudy and moody and overcast with a suggestion of storms in the afternoon.

William looks cloudy and moody and overcast, with a suggestion of storms in the afternoon.

I've brought John along (he said he wasn't up to anything special), and he currently has one of the boys (Twin No. 2) engaged in a long and detailed explanation as to how the use of a new plastic compound will revolutionise the processes of fuel extraction leading up to the turn of the century and that this is, ' . . . all really very, very interesting if you really look into it'.

Twin No. 2's glazed and slightly panicky eyes, his pained and distraught demeanour, suggest that he markedly fails to concur on that final point.

William and the other boys are standing out by the makeshift barbecue, disregarding the sausages and the chops and onion, and are engaged in a heated debate as to who was the best out of Henry the VIII's wives.

Curly argues that Catherine of Aragon showed all the most regal of queenly graces: a sound classical education, a competent administrator, adept at balancing the conflict of loyalty between her Iberian origins and her new realm, though he accepts she was probably a damn dud root.

William concurs that she was well educated, a sound administrator, balanced her mixed loyalties adeptly, and in fact reckons she would have gone off like a firecracker, but still reckons she was not a scratch on Catherine Parr.

Dibs is in his room sulking after his steadfast and impassioned advocacy of Anna of Cleves was met with hoots of derision and a bowl of fruit punch being poured over his head.

I say that I thought that Anne Boleyn was the prettiest:

— I think Anne Boleyn was the prettiest.

— Pretty in a fairly sluttish accessible kind of way.

Says William, genially enough, and in a way that suggests he considers my point interesting enough, and legitimate contribution to the debate, only if you don't know him.

— No. Pretty in a pretty kind of way.

— She looked like a lightbulb, Margaret.

— They all looked like lightbulbs back then, William. She just looked like a particularly pretty kind of lightbulb.

— She was a slut.

— She wasn't a slut.

— She was so a fucking slut.

— She wasn't a slut, William. She'd just had it with a fat, hairy alcoholic prick who completely subordinated her desires and feelings to his own.

William reads between my lines:

— Cunt the fuck off.

And he wanders off to get another beer.

While he's gone I resume watching this flitty little bitty of bimbolina called Jane Scarface or Jane Scarbuttocks or something as she bittles and jimps around William's place.

I've been watching her all afternoon, watching her over-talk to people and over-laugh at their jokes and over-nod, over-seriously at their observations, pretty much affirming herself as one of the key people at this barbecue. And I've watched her watching William. And I've watched him watching me.

When William returns from the kitchen he markedly stays at approximately ten paces from me until his seat is taken in his momentary absence by Jack and he is forced to sit on the bench beside me.

— What's the deal with the little blonde piece?

— Who, Jane? You were introduced.

— Yes. We were before. Who is she?

— I don't know. She's just the Jane thing. The thing that is Jane. Not your Jane.

— Oh derrhh, not my Jane. I did nearly mistake her for my sister whom I've known for fifteen years. Thanks for clearing that up. What's her deal?

— I don't know. She's just some chick.

— Well who died and made her Christmas?

— Look she's just a person. I don't know . . . she's just a nice person.

— Is she going out with one of the boys?

— No.

— Well what's her connection?

— I am actually. If that's okay. I know her from the Builders Arms. Met her the night I saw the Band of Hope gig and asked her along.

— Why?

— Why what?

— Why did you do that, William?

— Why did I what? Why did I meet her a couple of times? Because it was our first day at school and neither of us knew where the tuckshop was. Shit, Margaret.

— Why did you feel you had to have her here?

— Seemed like fun. Why did you have to bring John-shmohn?

— So let me get this straight . . . you thought it would be fun to have some little piece of popsicle-slut here, to have her flounce and flit around when all your friends

139

know she's your latest fuck, and I'm meant to just sit and grin it out. You're a cunt.

— Oh you've lost it, Margaret.

— And you're a cunt.

— Don't you think you're just making a few major quantum leaps here? Why is it that just because I know a person who happens to be female that I'm automatically . . .

— What's your point? What point are you trying to make having her here?

— Oh sweet Jesus. That the amount of water displaced by an object is equal to its surface area. That Churchill knew about Hiroshima in advance and that the connection between reality and your deranged insidious brain is a very fucking muddled and twisted line.

— She's ugly.

— I wouldn't know.

— She's so thin she looks sick.

— Is that a fact?

— She looks anorexic.

— Maybe she doesn't stuff her face with two plates of potato salad at Grand Final barbecues before the meat's even been served.

— Fuck you. I'll eat whatever I want.

— Blue whales and herds of buffalo be warned. Margaret's feeling a bit peckish.

— Fuck you. She looks like a concentration camp survivor.

William pauses, and then with smooth and deliberate 'fuck you' cockiness says:

— She's actually got a slight pot belly.

— You arsehole.

— I only know because she told me she can't get a belly button ring.

— As if.

— In the real world that's a perfectly logical and accept-
able reason for me knowing about her tummy but it just
doesn't run in your fucked brain.

— As fucking if.

— Grow up.

— Screw you.

— Get a life.

— Fuck you.

— Is this turning you on?

— What?

— Fuck me.

— Fuck you.

— Fuck me, Margaret.

— Not a chance.

— Please.

— Not this time.

— No. Not this time. I wouldn't want to waste the come.

At this point John tentatively tip-toes up to me and says:

— Um . . . Margaret . . . I was wondering if you'd like
or felt like another drink.

He passes the Sub Zero to me and as I take it William
stares at the bottle and his whole visage clouds over and
he turns cadaverous pale.

He stares at me and then finishes his can of beer. Then
with little passion, but thoughtfully, he whispers:

— I'm sorry. I know we both get caught up in this whole
vindictive kind of thing and neither of us knows how to
stop it. I'm sorry. I do love you and I think . . . I know
you love me. I'm really, really sorry. Oh . . . and one
further thing . . . sometimes I almost wish I had AIDS just
so I'd know that I'd been pumping that death shit into
you.

He stands up and grabs my drink and smashes it against
the wall of next door's metalworks factory. Then he goes
into the house. Everyone stares at me and I say 'It had a

fucking snail in it', and then after five minutes when I've stopped shaking I follow him up into the house.

He's not in the kitchen and I'm too scared to go any further. I need to cool down. He needs to cool down. Jane Scarbum has followed me in and her mouth starts making sounds:

— Are you okay? That looked really full-on out there. I'm really sorry if you and William are having a blue. You seem like a really, really nice person. Are you okay? Can I get you a cup of tea?

Then I watch, disempowered, as she floats and bustles busily around the kitchen and rhythmically goes straight from the coffee and tea cupboard, without pausing or checking, to the canister with the sugar in it (the one with SAGO written on it) to the mug cupboard, instinctively moves aside William's mug (the one with the picture of the prim newfoundland dog on it) to get at the all purpose anyone/guest mugs at the back, and then sets up all the different elements on the chopping board.

Then she lifts up her pretty Lisa Ho skirt, shows me her vagina and says, 'Margaret hon. I love it when your boy-friend puts his penis in my pussy.'

Not the last bit actually. But she may as well have. It's effectively what she'd done.

She looks around at me, registers me staring at her open-mouthed and says (her mantra obviously):

— Are you okay?
— What's your poxy little name?
— Um . . . it's Jane.
— Oh.
— Are you okay?
— Jane . . . honey . . . you know where everything is.
— What?
— You know absolutely where absolutely everything is in this kitchen. It's just kind of a bit in my face, that's all.

142

Jane pauses, and looks down embarrassed. She notices a ball of fluff that has settled in the centre of the gerbera she wears pinned on her cheery little left breast. Then, faltering, she says:

— Margaret. I'm really, really sorry. I know how important you are to William and I'm sorry that I might have been . . . I really felt that I was there for him at a time when he really needed someone to talk to and I was happy to be there because I think he's a really beautiful person. If I can talk to you, just female to female, I know he really, really loves you and I really believe that you guys can . . .

— Jane, really, it's okay. I know that you and him have had this thing going.

— I'm sorry.

— Well I didn't actually *know* but you've pretty much just confirmed it. Anyway, it's no stress.

— I'm sorry.

And hearing her say that again blew it for me. I said:

— Hon . . . it doesn't matter. I knew William had been seeing someone, he mentioned this girl who had this problem, and I pretty much figure it must have been you after being in your vicinity for about one minute, and honestly Jane, female to female, I know that there's a hell of a lot of good feminine hygiene sprays and cleansing soaps that could really, really help you.

I wander up the hall.

William

Margaret timidly knocks on the door, and then creeps into my room, biting her lip and standing nervous like she's frightened of me.

Like she's scared of me.

Like she's worried about what I might do.

Get lost.

Don't dump this shit on me. I mightn't be much but at least I have never touched or hit or hurt you. Don't play the 'I'm scared of the big intimidating male' crap. You know I have never done anything like that.

This is William here.

This is William who you have gone out with for six months or something and I have never hurt you or anything.

I find this insulting.

— So?

   — So what?

   — So that was quite a display, William.

   — What?

   — The throwing the bottle against the wall.

   — I thought it would look pretty all smashing and . . .

   — It did.

   — Cool. So who's winning?

   — What?

   — Who's winning in the football?

   — Not sure. Are Carlton playing?

   — Could be.

   — Do we like them?

   — They're okay.

   — I think they're winning then.

Margaret

William fiddles with a paperweight in the shape of an ascending Sputnik.

   — William . . .

— Margaret . . .

— We're pretty much fucked up at the moment, aren't we?

— How 'bout we forget it all then?

— What do you mean?

— Just forget it. Forget the whole relationship thing. Throw the towel in. You can piss off and I'll have a good life.

— Is that what you want? Is that the best plan you can think of?

— It's not really up to me is it?

— Of course it's up to you, William.

— Sure.

— Well you're the one setting the scene.

— Margaret if I was setting this scene it'd have dinosaurs and space ships in it. And balloons. This is some crap you've come up with.

— William . . .

— Look . . . why are you still talking to me?

— I had a nice chat to Jane.

— If by Jane you mean a triceratops in a Tie Fighter I'm happy to listen. Otherwise . . .

— By Jane I mean the woman you're currently sleeping with.

Pause.

— I'm . . . not.

— Oh William for God's sake you're busted. You're sprung. You fucked up. Just face up to it.

— I don't want to talk about it.

— Care factor zero. I do want to talk about it.

— Well . . . I really don't, Margaret.

— So we'll just leave it. Just break up. Throw it all away. Is that really what you want? Is that really what you think? Talk to me.

— No, Margaret.

— You're useless.

— Fuck yourself.

— Well just quietly, William, I'd be giving myself the best sex I've had in half a year.

— Well I'm sure me and all the other guys who have been through you will take that to heart.

— Don't try to turn this around on to me. You're the one who's been busted.

— Don't push it.

— There haven't been any other guys. I wish.

— Really, Margaret . . . leave it.

— You haven't got anything on me.

— I know more than you think.

— You know shit.

— I know that you and John have got the same pass-out stamps on your wrist.

William

Without thinking she immediately looks down at her wrist and instinctively rubs it with her thumb.

— I don't care about you lying to me, Margaret, and telling me you wanted an early night and then pissing off with John, but at least have the style to make sure you've both washed the bloody stamps off your wrists before you turn up here.

Margaret looks down at her wrist again, pauses, looks up and over my shoulder. I can see her brain racing away behind her eyes. Then she looks at me and says:

— Get over it, loser.

I didn't get that. It took me a moment to understand that. She looks at me earnestly and in complete innocence. What actually is the . . . correct face or expression to have when you're breaking someone else's heart? Is it a smile or a frown or completely blank? I did not deserve this. And you're breaking my heart, Margaret. I looked at her for a while . . . stared and watched over and remembered her . . . remembered her body . . . remembered us. What did she do with us? Why did she kill us? Us. Of all people.

Someone else tell this next bit.

Margaret

Pretty much this is about the point where he punched me in the face. I fell backwards and stumbled gracelessly back onto his couch. I held carefully, and tried to rework my jaw, and with my fingers mopped up the blood seeping from my mouth.

He watches me confused, not yet sure that his last action is responsible for what's happened to me and why I've got blood now streaming from my mouth. Not yet logging on to why I'm now screaming in pain and terror and not sure why people are bashing insistently at the door.

He's looking frantic, looking for someone to accuse and to blame, and somewhere to hide.

I will miss you, William, and I will love you and remember you till the day I die. But you are a seriously fucked young man. You have done the 'Margaret Palmer experience'. I hope it brought you some small joy. Goodbye, William. And I really hope you suffer a long time in hell. I say:

— A. I didn't even fuck John. I am allowed to have male friends, you know.

— B. Don't ever hit me again. You do not hit women, you fuckwit.

— C. I did fuck John.

147

— and D. You're a fuckwit.

And that's when I walked out. Slamming the door behind me. I guess I love or loved William. But fuck him, I'm allowed to have male friends. That is permitted. So fuck him for all his possessive, proprietorial shit.

Fuck you, William.

Fuck you, you cunt.

Piss off.

William

There should be a day, an international day, when we're all allowed to redesign that one object or thing that causes us the greatest despair and distress.

And on that day, that day of amnesty and redesign, the male kitchen-hands can move the sinks up about six or seven inches, the writers can put the 'A' in typewriters over and into the middle, and the arachnophobics can make the spiders yellow and cute and fluffy. On that day the chickens and lambs and cows and pigs can make themselves less tasty, the Irish and Scots and Welsh can make England sink, and Alan Alda and Bob Hoskins and Michelle Pfeiffer can make all the copies and all the prints of *Sweet Liberty* buckle and burn and disappear.

And on that day I'm going to redesign answering machines because I am sick to death of coming home to that one, unblinking red eye. I'm sick of blundering around the house and wanting to call her and steeling myself not to call her. Wanting her to call and knowing she's not going to call. Leaving the house, walking in tears to the supermarket, dawdling and delaying and loitering, and willing her to have called in my absence. Coming home to that unblinking, burning red answer. The answering machine feigning ignorance and looking up at me in open-eyed innocence: 'What? Was someone meant to call? I didn't know that. Who was meant to call?'

We need an answering machine that as soon as you enter the house shouts gleefully:

'No one called. Fuck You.

'She didn't call. Fuck You.

'You're all alone. Fuck You.

'She's over you. Fuck You.

'You matter shit. Fuck You.'

Margaret

I feel like an iron band has been stripped from my eyes and now I can start winking at people.

An iron mask that had crocodile grips that dragged my brow into a frown, that had needles that dug into my eyes, and weights that pulled my mouth down to a glum line has been removed and I can see sunshine.

Jane has peppered me with questions and quizzed me as to why and how and how permanent the break-up is and then added as an after thought that she wishes me well.

And John has courted me earnestly.

I miss you, William.

At your best you were wonderful and I wish you well.

But I'm over you.

Get over me.

William

Monday.

Worst so far.

Despair/Anguish equals greater than Resolve/Determination.

Buckled at 2.10.

Called her at her new flat.

Got answering machine.

Redialled another seven times.

Love your voice.

Wish someone could filter to me some rotten news. That they saw you having sex with seven football teams and a badminton player.

Wish I could get angry. Wish I could hate you. Wish I could find a reason for us breaking up or at least believe in and hold with the eighty or so ones that I've got.

Can't.

I wish I could hate you.

Don't.

Love you.

Margaret

It's Monday and tonight's gone fairly well . . .

I had the folks come around and meet J and see my new flat all set up.

They bought me one of those large glass pasta jars with the cork.

I wish J didn't get along with Dad so well. I'm nervous about that theory that women marry men like their fathers.

I wish Jane wasn't such a smart-arse. If she'd only give J a chance.

Now I'm thinking I might release my answering machine message on CD.

Looks like I'd have at least one buyer.

J's cock is odd. Odd bend. Weird.

William.

Sunday—
   Mixed.
   Morning—pretty bleak.
   Afternoon—fucked and unbearable until nap.
   Night—
   Blade Runner—despair containable.
   The China Syndrome—struggling but holding on.
   Carry On Abroad—pissed on scotch and in tears.
   Margaret!!

Margaret

I wish someone would fuck William and get him off my
case. It's just that we weren't right for each other.
   I was bad for you.
   There'll be someone else really neat and nice and fun.
   Don't torture yourself like this.
   I don't hate you, or at least don't address hating you. If
you could just do what I'm doing and realise what an
opportunity this represents.
   It's fun out here.
   Get a life.
   It's over.

William

I really have to do something to seal and close and finish
this part of my life. To start the next chapter.

Margaret

You really have to do something to put this behind you.

William

Help me, Margaret.

Margaret

Get help, toss-pot.

William

And this is a phone call that I made.

— [Deep voice] Yes hello. This is . . . Peter Ferguson. I wonder, could I please speak to ah . . . Ms ah . . . Ms Jane Palmer.

— This is Jane Palmer. Who the fuck's Peter Ferguson?

— Oh Jane. Hello Jane. It's um . . . it's actually um . . . William. William Casey. Um . . . how are you?

— I'm good . . . I guess. Yeah . . . I'm fine. Do you want Margaret?

— Well yeah, sure. I suppose um . . . is she there?

— No she's not actually. She doesn't live here any more.

— Well, I know. I just thought . . . she might be . . .

— I can tell her you called.

— That'd be great . . .

— You could try her at her flat. The number's . . .

— Yeah . . . yeah. I'll do that . . . I've got the actual number . . . um . . .

— I'll tell her you rang.
— Okay. Thanks, Jane. That'd be good. Um . . . Jane . . .
— Yes?
— Oh . . . nothing. How's school?
— Okay, I guess.
— Good. That's good. Okay. I'll speak to you soon.
— Goodnight William.
— Thanks, Jane. Goodnight.

This is another call I made about a minute later. No actually . . . I'll time this. I owe you nothing if not accuracy. I hung up the phone, finished a glass of scotch, and pressed redial on the phone. One Mississippi, Two Mississippi, Three Mississippi, Four Mississippi, Five Mississippi, Six Cat and Dog, Seven Mississippi, Eight Mississippi, Nine Mississippi . . .
— Hello?
— Hello Jane. William again . . .

Nine seconds. Actually nine seconds. Not a minute but actually nine seconds later. This is a second phone call I made approximately nine seconds later.

— Hello?
— Hello, Jane. William again . . .
— William. How are you? William . . . what's this all about?
— Jane, I have absolutely no idea.
— You're fretting?
— I am fretting something shocking.
— And you're uptight?
— I'm redefining the word.
— And you're stressed?
— I'm taking it to new dimensions.
— And I guess you're pretty pissed.

— Considerably.

— Well?

— Well . . .

— Well, she's not here. She doesn't live here.

— No. I know. I know she's not. I called to just . . .

— William . . .

— What?

— William . . . I think you and Margaret have hit a rough patch.

— I know. I know we have.

— You know she's been hooking around with John quite a bit.

— I know. I'm just . . . I've just called to . . .

— Called to?

— I don't know.

— To just say Hi?

— I guess . . .

— To say Hi to me?

— Maybe. I think so. I'm not sure. To say Hi to somebody . . .

— Well . . . you've got me.

— I suppose I have.

— Well?

— Well . . . Hi, Jane.

— Hi, William. How are you?

— I'm really not well. Not well at all.

— Are you really very, very drunk?

— I'm really very, very considerably.

— Are you happy?

— I'm falling apart. You?

— I don't know. Shit, I'm fine. William . . . what are you doing?

— No idea. It's not just me.

— Well it kind of is.

154

— Well it's kind of not Jane. Did you ever . . . have you ever . . . when you used to call me . . .

— To get Margaret.

— Jane . . .

— What?

— You kind of had a schoolgirl crush on me, yes? It's not . . . just me.

— No. It's not just you.

— I'm kind of handsome, yes?

— Not . . . really.

— Cute?

— In an uncute way.

— Sexy?

— You're . . . Why are you asking me this?

— I . . .

— Well, William. What happens now?

— Jane . . . I'm not sure. Honey, I'm just not sure. I think it involves books.

— Books, William?

— I think so.

— How so?

— I think you ask me what's a good book to read at the moment.

— What's a good book to read at the moment?

— *John Dollar*.

— And?

— *The Maypole*.

— And?

— And that's where it starts.

— Really, William, I really think that's where it finishes.

— Jane . . . this is not just me.

— I really think you're a bit drunk.

— This is not just me.

— Call tomorrow.

— Does Margaret talk about me?

— Call tomorrow.

— I'm sorry, Jane . . .

— Just leave it.

— I really wasn't that bad by her . . .

— You rang to talk to me about my fucking big sister?

— I'm sorry.

— Call tomorrow.

— Don't be like your big sister.

— Fuck you. Get off the fucking phone.

— I just . . . I just needed someone to talk to . . . and you . . .

— William . . . I think it's best if you just forget it and sleep on it and see what tomorrow feels like.

— I'm sorry, Jane. This is a lot to put on you.

— William . . .

— What?

— You and Margaret are over.

— I know that.

— William . . .

— What?

— Call tomorrow.

— I think about you a lot, Jane.

— William . . .

— What?

— Can you do an essay for me?

Margaret

I'm thinking about you a lot, boy.

I'm thinking about you a lot.

I'm thinking about . . . William. There is a point that every person reaches in their life . . . every person . . . not just the high school drop-outs and the middle-class losers, but

156

everyone. Everyone must one day seize their life. Yes . . . I dreamt of being a princess.

I thought I was going to discover the cure for cancer.

I believed that one day I'd colonise Mars.

I hoped that one day I'd be Penelope Pitstop in the Pink Pussycat and beat Dick Dastardly (and fuck Peter Perfect in the fields of France).

But it's just not going to happen that way.

It's not going to happen. This is not my beautiful life . . . but it's my life. It's as good as it gets.

It's reality.

It's all we've got.

And we want you here.

William, you have been the biggest arsehole I have ever encountered and I so loathe and despise you but . . . it'd be nice if you could show us what berries we can eat, and what birds fly to water and which flowers make the sun rise.

You can help us.

I miss you.

Come here, William.

William

I got a parcel in my letter box. A parcel about the size of a book, if by that you're thinking about a book the size of a hardcover new release novel as opposed to a book about the size of a dictionary or the size of a lorry. A parcel about the size of a book that's about the size of a video tape.

It's a parcel wrapped in a padded mustard-coloured envelope and is addressed to myself with a sticky label that's been printed out from a computer with a mail-list function.

The parcel which contains something which is about the size of a book that's approximately the size of a video tape, contains a video tape. On the slip cover are written the words 'My Family' and I know it is definitely in Jane Palmer's handwriting even though I don't think I've ever seen Jane's handwriting.

Before we proceed can we just momentarily digress. I've just re-read this and it seems unlikely. What's about to happen seems unlikely. When I told my sister, when we had one of our conversations where I tried to shock and impress her with the comparatively wild and unruly life-style I lead after years of being the golden child who shone against the foil of her sinister existence, she said:

— Did that really happen? It seems unlikely.

When I told the other boys, and when I acquiesced to their demands to see the actual video in question, which I showed them until that last and final scene, they said:

— I really didn't think you were being serious. I really thought you were having us on. It seemed so unlikely.

When I showed Angela, she of the Gallic Orgasm, my best female friend and confidante, she said:

— I really didn't believe you. I would never have had the presumption or temerity to hazard something like that at that age. This is a remarkable young woman. It seemed so unlikely.

This is a remarkable young woman.

That's why I'm telling you this story. There are parts of this story I deem worthy of bringing to public attention, and Jane is one of them. So bear with me.

See . . . if you can believe and accept that one small white boy can free and emancipate the black people of South Africa by bashing the shit out of one of their own then you can believe what I'm saying.

If you can accept and unquestioningly receive that one peculiar and bland Greenlandian woman called Ms. Smilla can approach and achieve orgasm by pressing her clitoris against the opened hole of some fellow's penis then accept and reserve your incredulity that this video was sent to me.

This is absolutely true.

Jane is a remarkable woman.

These were remarkable times.

This video exists.

I have it hidden in my room and re-stickered with a label that says 'Sweet Liberty (A. Alda, B. Hoskins)', so as to ensure that no one ever thinks to watch it.

This happened.

I'll return to our story.

I'm home alone and I put the video on and it starts with Jane sitting cross-legged on the ground with 'My Family' written beside her, arranged out on the dirt next to her with different-length sticks, and changing from upper-case to lower-case at random. She has used a sea shell for the letter A, and even though it isn't shaped like an A (or an a), it doesn't matter because it was never going to be a C or a Q or the number 2. There is no volume.

In the next scene they're all there except for Jane.

It must be something like a Christmas or a birthday or Easter or something because there's a grandmother or two and a cousin.

They are standing on the verandah of the Palmers' house.

I see. Jane was setting up the video on the tripod because she now comes into view and joins them, on the porch, and puts two fingers up behind Margaret's head doing the old 'donkey ears' trick.

The scene changes. Tootles, the Palmers' golden labrador, is sitting, squatting in their backyard. His legs are

159

shaking slightly, his whole body shivering as he strains to move his bowels. He's looking up, over to the left past the camera, and is clearly concentrating. After a few moments his whole body relaxes and he straightens, and wanders off out of view.

Mr Palmer is sitting on a banana lounge reading a newspaper in their backyard. It's the Sunday *Herald-Sun*. He subtly edges up onto his side, rising up one of his arse cheeks, holds there for a moment, and then rests back down. After a moment he frowns, inhales deeply, winces and then fans his immediate vicinity with the newspaper. He looks up, sees the camera, blushes, and then covers his face with the newspaper.

The next scene is of me. I don't know where I am. Oh . . .

The camera pans back and I'm sitting by the side of the Palmers' pool with my legs hanging in the water. I lean forward, and pick up a tennis ball out of the water and throw it across the pool and Tootles runs on and chases it into the bushes.

I look like a bit of a spunk, actually.

Next scene is the backyard of the Palmers' again. From how I figure it, Jane must have had the camera just peeping out from behind their garage where they keep a few rakes and brooms and the compost bin. I don't know why she's gone to all the trouble of putting the camera there because it's all really cramped and grotty and there's heaps of spider webs and shit. So right at the start she's got us looking straight up the yard at the back fence, and then it starts panning around to the left slowly and we see the clothesline (there's a few items hanging on it and I think that blue thing was one of Mr Palmer's singlets), their garden furniture (white wrought-iron seats and a table that looks slightly rococo in a garden furniture type way), the barbecue (a large brick sturdy structure with a wooden side bit that houses the large, white gas bottle), the start of the pool (better than a beach in your own backyard), my arse popping up and down (testicles jiggling madly and the underside of my penis sliding up and down into Margaret's vagina), a wheelbarrow, the side of the house, and then the hose and sprinkler gathered up beside the back door. The camera pans back and settles on my arse which is still humping up and down. Then I sit down on my haunches and Margaret lifts herself up, we kiss for a few moments, she gently pushes me down, so I'm lying on my back, and she squats over me, her hands on my chest, quivering, and rising and lowering herself on my penis.

She looks not unlike Tootles when he was having a crap.

The scene changes and we see again Tootles having a crap.

The next scene is inside. The camera takes a moment to adjust to the darkness and then reveals Jane's bedroom. It pans around the room and then comes to the door and focuses on her shoes and socks dumped messily on the floor. We leave her room and are going along the hallway stopping to take note of her school jumper lying on the floor and then her school shirt. At the door to her parents' bedroom is her school skirt. It's the traditional blue gingham and lying crumpled next to the doorframe, half in half out, and as we turn and enter Mr and Mrs Palmer's bedroom we can see that the door to the en suite is slightly open and there are clouds of steam coming from within. We move forward and the camera lowers down and focuses for a few moments and lingers on her underpants and her small white bra (It looks like it's only just been discarded. Just delicately sitting there and looking up, the sides and straps curling up like fern fronds, and still warm from the body of its wearer. Steaming.) . . . lying about a foot apart before the door to the en suite.

The picture stops, just for a second. (I figure Jane has had to set the camera on a tripod and get into the shower. I think that's where this scene is heading. I shift for a moment in the chair, easing the pressure on myself, stretching out my legs.)

We can see the bathroom, it's thick with steam and behind the clouded glass doors to the shower a vague figure, about Jane's height, is moving behind the glass. This person washing themself, I can see one arm is up and the other is rubbing underneath it. A pink hand becomes clear and distinct as it settles on the glass, finds the handle, I draw breath sharply, and then the sliding doors are pulled open.

Jane waves and dances at the camera wearing a wet suit, swimming mask and a snorkel.

Then this scene.

The television goes blank for about three seconds, and then we're outside in the Palmers' backyard, and Jane is sitting looking straight into the camera. It's a cold, overcast day. I can see the wind is blowing the trees in the background, and is lightly blowing on Jane, moving through her hair. She is sitting at the furniture by the pool, but close to the camera, we can see just from her waist up to her head. She has her back to the camera but has turned her torso around so as she's facing directly into . . . facing . . . looking straight at me, and hence her body, her breasts are in profile . . .

I turn the video off and leave the house. I'm out of here.

I'm out in the backyard and I'm putting my hands on the back of my neck and stretching and letting the cold wind blow against me and . . .

I'm stuffing stray bits of straw in through the chicken wire of the guinea pig cage and . . .

Things are looming up on me. Things are conjoining and planets are lining up and the whole universe is colluding and conspiring and setting itself in place for this moment and events are moving into this situation where . . .

I can hear the video singing.

I can hear the sirens calling me from the rocks as we sail by their shore and I'm strapping myself to this mast and I . . .

You are so beautiful, Jane, and I am so . . . you are a very beautiful woman.

And I am very much your older sister's former boy-friend and you are very young.

> Ay, no; no, ay; for I must nothing be;
> Therefore no, no, for I resign to thee.
> Now mark me how I will undo myself.
>> Richard II.

I am desperately attracted to Jane Palmer.

Frantically.

Madly.

I love thee to the depth + breadth + height my soul can reach and can't . . . can't have her.

She is divine.

And I cannot have her, cannot have her.

The very thought is repulsive to . . . is not repulsive . . . the thought is glorious, but . . .

How can I impress upon you the grave beauty of this woman–child this part-teen part-goddess. The . . . I cannot have her.

She is a beautiful woman.

She is a little girl.

I am purifying myself.

Purging myself of base and impure desires.

I am cleansing myself of all that is sleazy and seedy and greedy and base.

I'm thinking about kittens.

Sweet and happy little kittens.

I am not a creepy horny big fellow with a lust thing happening for someone who is young enough to be . . . well . . . too young.

I'm a kitten-liker.

Cute, little kittens.

Sweet little greeting-card kittens.

Laughing and rolling around on the soft plush carpet as the warm afternoon sun shines in through the sitting-room window.

Tossing and pushing around a large red ball of wool and thwacking at it with their sweet and pure, cute little paddy paws.

Miaow Miaow.

Happy little kittens.

Completely unaware that just outside the window, just outside is a large mongrel, battle-scarred alley cat watching their play, watching their innocence . . . moaning around and now rubbing his erect cat cock against the ground and waiting for the moment to, the chance to push his way through the half open window and stuff his . . .

I'm thinking about smurfs. Happy smurfs.

Happy little blue smurfs giggling and singing and wandering across hills.

Pure smurfs.

And Puff the Magic Dragon.

And Bambi.

And Dumbo.

And there's bluebird and Charlie Brown ('How's the baseball going? You keep at it'), and a happy smiling Garfield ('Easy on the lasagne buddy'), and there's a smurf building a happy little smurf letterbox ('Ho ho. Hope you don't get too many bills my smurf friend'), and there's you know, the pink, the snagglepuss or someone, and there's the Little Mermaid, her tight little pert breasts pushing against the shell bra and one bead of water just slowly coursing down past her navel, down and then I'm standing next to her I pull her up by the arm and put my hand on her tit and firmly rub it, can feel the nipple harden under . . .

Not the Little Mermaid. Not her. No. I'm thinking about Pinocchio and Jabber Jaw and the . . . those little munchkin mushrooms from Fantasia and the Crocodile from Peter Pan and Captain Hook and you know in the Disney film the kid that was the youngest of the Darling Boys and the way they flew through the night sky of London and Smee and Tinkerbell when she's standing on the mirror and she checks the width of her thighs and runs her hands up and down and then she's trapped in the sewing drawer in the Nursery and she tries to get out through the keyhole and she gets stuck halfway and I can see her legs are spread out and braced against the side of the drawer and she's struggling and wriggling and her skirt rises up and shows her firm tight little arse in those sweet little lemon knickers and her arse is pushing and pulling back and forwards, back and forwards, riding up and down on my coc . . .

I'm thinking about smurfs.

I'm thinking about fuckin' hundreds of the blue fucking little fucking smurf fucks. Oh they're cute. I love 'em.

Village party fun jump jump leap.

Oh and look who's visiting Smurfland—

There's the Care Bears and Muppets and My Little Pony and Barb . . . Masters of the Universe and Hurry Hungry Hippos and the . . . the . . . . you know . . . bloody bloody Baloo and Bristow and there's the Flintstones and Barney and Pebbles . . . you know like when she's grown up and she's got these fucking legs that just go on and on and that tight little pussy of hers is just begging for . . .

Fucking smurfs shit god god Jane get out of my head.

Jane get out of my head.

The wire door crashes loudly as I crash my way through the small washhouse-cum-rear-landing. The couch shifts slightly on its legs when I dump myself upon it. The remote control can barely stifle its giggles as I search the room for it while it hides slipped down between the cushions of the couch. The play button looks slightly stained and marked by its more frequent usage than the other command functions as I press my thumb down on it. The video clicks and junks itself into motion, finding the tape and flicking once and then a second time, and then filling the screen and my world with Jane.

She's wearing a fawn shirt, I think perhaps like the one Margaret has, and the first few buttons are undone, so it's slightly open and I can see one of . . . one of her breasts . . . it's the one that would be further from the camera.

She is not wearing a bra.

Her nipple is very dark and erect, the cold I think, and she has three small brown spots on her breast, just over her nipple.

Jane has the clock on the video for this scene and at its start it shows 00:00:00 in the bottom left hand corner of my television screen.

By 00:00:06 I have taken my tracksuit pants off.

At 00:0:42 Jane frowns and bites her bottom lip for three seconds and then widens her eyes and gives a half smile which she holds until 00:00:54.

At 00:01:30 she turns her head and looks away from the camera, is in full profile then turns back to look at me again and blinks sharply.

At 00:02:20 a wisp of her hair falls forward, down over her eyes and she lifts it up and out of the way and runs her hand through her hair and down the back, and holds and gently rubs the back of her neck and then she smiles again from 00:02:35 to 00:02:38.

At 00:03:14 the wind blows against her shirt, pressing it against her body, and she looks down and undoes another button and lifts and opens her neckline up again so as I can still see her bust and she . . . runs her hand across the fabric, and then rests, just sets her hand against the underside of her breast, cups it and lifts up slightly and regards it for a moment and then looks back at the camera.

At 00:03:57 I come and the semen falls on my leg and some falls on my thumb and some lands heavily on the carpet.

At 00:04:00 the screen goes black.

Um . . .

Just Um really. That's all. Um.

Um . . . what are you doing tomorrow, um . . . you know . . . today was a bugger of a day . . . um, how are you sort of thing?

You know . . . just um.

Um.

The um thing.

William

Then this.

At this point I'm alone in the house (the boys are off somewhere kicking around a football or playing hide-n-seek or getting pissed), sitting cross-legged on the floor of my bedroom with my deck of playing cards set out before me on the matted and grubbed carpet, playing a game of patience; a particularly formatted form of patience that I had only that weekend learned from my sister and brother-in-law.

I'm not winning here.

Not winning at all.

I don't mean I'm not winning at cards. In fact I've successfully completed thirteen rounds of the game with no default and I am beginning to figure that in some way I have misunderstood the rules.

I mean I'm not winning at life.

And I'm not winning at getting over you.

And I'm not winning at missing you.

Margaret, I'm fucking missing you but I'm finding a way of not missing you.

I'm trying to sleep as much as possible because when I'm asleep an hour or three can pass without this enormous grief and sorrow that is every moment spent awake. I can't open a can of spaghetti or watch a video or open a door without pausing in a shudder of tears.

Oh Margaret. I'm sorry. I'm sorry about your jaw, honey. I'm sorry that I . . . I'm sorry about whatever happened to your . . .

And I'm sorry about me.

I miss you.

In sleep I still miss you, and dream of you and mourn you, but occasionally in my dreams I fuck you and hold you and am with you and that's just not here when I'm awake.

And yes admittedly sometimes I'm just something completely unlikely like a Jam Baker with a charming store and a dear friend who's a talking yellow dog called Roy.

Flab, flab, flab.

Flip, flip, flip.

The cards are set out before me again, and in this pursuit and endeavour, another five minutes will be passed and then another five and then another five and then I can think about watching *Wheel of Fortune* and then I'll get pissed and go to bed. And I hope I won't have called you.

Blank,Blank,Blank,Blank,Blank,Blank,Blank,Blank.
Blank,Blank,Blank,Blank,Blank,Blank,Blank,Blank.
Eight,King,Ace,Two,Queen,Jack,Two,Three.
Ten,Queen,Eight,Jack,Ten,Four,Nine.
Four,Five,Seven,Six,Six,Eight.
Five,Four,Queen,King,Jack.
Seven,Seven,Queen,Five.
Nine,Ace,Five.
Six,Ace.
Queen.

This is boring me.

Do something.

This is boring me.

Move the six onto the seven and the four onto the five.

This is boring me.

Now you can move that Ace up to the top.

This is so dull.

Point being, at this moment when I'm playing cards, just playing patience and waiting for 'Wheel' to start, the doorbell is pressed, and I leap up and catch my foot under the base of the wardrobe door that is hanging open and stumble forward a few paces, I lumber up the hallway, on the way trying to discern the identity of the slightly small silhouette of the person that shifts and changes and shudders behind the nubilated glass set in our front door and say:

— Yes hello . . . who's there?

And they say:

— Jane.

Or rather, not *they* but *she* says:

— Jane.

Jane's here.

She. Her. At my house. Pressing my door buzzer. At my place. Here.

Now.

Get away.

Come here.

— Hello.

— What do you want? Margaret's not here.

— I'm wagging school. I came around for a coffee or something.

So I pat down my hair and try to muss it into correct form and quickly survey the hallway and what I can see of the house and consider vacuuming and washing the walls and gathering up the newspapers and dusting (which incidentally, I don't even think we have the apparatus for), and then am interrupted from my honourable and domestically noble contemplations by my hand which despite my inattention has been busy opening the front door. I can see Jane. HER appearance silhouetted in my doorframe, silhouetted in my doorframe, my doorframe, holding her heavy school bag over her shoulder, and looking at me (ME) as I say:

— Well this is a nice surprise. How are you, Jane?

And she comes in and slides past me who is standing idle dumb-struck in the hallway and walks purposefully down the hallway and drops her school bag in the middle of the sitting room and sits down and I say:

— Do you want a coffee?

No, sorry. Typo error.

That was meant to be:

AND *SHE* COMES INTO MY MY *MY* HOUSE AND DROPS *HER* SCHOOL BAG AND SITS DOWN AND GRACES MY HALL AND MY HOUSE AND MY SURROUNDINGS AND MY WORLD WITH *HER*.

The her.

She's in my house.

HERE.

Jane's here.

— So, William. What do you do when you're just bumming around?

— When I'm bumming around? I stomp around this dumb house and smoke cigarettes and pass wind and at 4.30 I start drinking beer.

— Is this your bedroom?

She goes through the door and I answer:

— Kind of.

— So this is where you and my big sister fucked.

— Shit, Jane, you really are bad news sometimes.

— I've seen you fucking, you know that. She does go on a bit.

— Can we not discuss it? Do you want a coffee or a tea or something?

— Yeah, I'll have a coffee. White, two sugars. No, actually. Drop the sugars. No sugar. It's a real little kids thing to have two sugars in your coffee. How should I have my coffee, William? How do women have their coffee?

— I don't know. Out of a cup. You really shouldn't be wagging school.

— A long black? A flat white? A caffè latte? What's the right way to have my coffee? What's the right image? You're a grown-up. Tell me. A short black with a book of poetry and a table overlooking the Seine River? A café au lait please, with a beret and a mysterious past. Is that right? How does Margaret have her coffee?

— She drinks hot Milo.

— That'd be right. She's such a 'Margaret'.

— I'll get your coffee. Two sugars with a smartie face on top.

I go into my small kitchen and put the kettle on. Jane is so confident, so cocky. There is something going on here that I'm picking up on . . . She speaks with the assurance of a person who is resolutely set on a task, but just slightly underneath the bravado I can hear a slight waver, a nervous uncertainty. She yells at me from the bedroom:

— And this is where you fucked my big sister. I hope you were careful. God you would have that bloody photo of the rhino in the boat. Everyone has got that.

— I like rhinos.

— Everyone likes rhinos this year. Just like thirty years ago everyone liked puppies playing pool. Where's those goddamned people kissing in France?

— 'Le Baiser de l'Hôtel de Ville, Paris.' I don't have it.

— Well that's a fucking relief. It's not a bad photograph, but it's been done to death.

— It's a shocking photo, Jane.

— Did you know that's me in that picture? I'm the girl being kissed. I've just finished reading *Blue Eyes, Black Hair* by Marguerite Duras, and drunk my macchiato when Simeon from the French Underground meets me and

173

pushes the vital microfilm into my mouth with his lusty tongue.

— How do you know about Marguerite Duras?

— Shmargaret reads her.

Jane has come into the kitchen.

— God you're messy, William. Slob.

She goes back into the bedroom.

— You know, actually I'm not the woman in the photo. I'm the guy in the beret watching them. I'm watching them kiss and knowing that I'll never be in love like that. And that's you and Margaret kissing and I'm wishing it was me.

!?!

I've poured the coffees and take them, pausing at the door to my bedroom.

— You look fucked today.

— Ta.

Jane is sitting up on my bed, sitting up on her knees and pushing her hands down on her lap. She's rocking lightly, an easy back and forth. She asks:

— Are you edgy or something?

— No. Do you want to watch telly?

— Fuck telly.

— Here's your coffee.

— Fuck coffee.

— Do you want to go to the park?

— Fuck the park.

— Do you want to call your mother?

— Fuck my . . . No, I don't.

— You swear too much.

— I only say Fuck. And not as a swear word. I say it as in 'Fuck'. To Fuck. Fucking. They Fucked. She Fucked. He Fucked. We Fucked. I haven't ever Fucked. It's not my word yet.

— Can I take you to see a film?

— Why?

— I don't know, Jane. Let's just go and see a movie.

— No.

— Well, do you want to go roller-skating?

— Roller-skating?

— Well I don't know, Jane. You're wagging school. Aren't we meant to roller-skate or go to a park and smoke cigarettes and then go shoplifting?

— I'm not a kid.

— You're fifteen.

— Actually, I'm thirty-four. I stopped ageing physically when I saw my parents killed by the Gestapo.

— You're just a kid.

— I'm a young woman.

— Can we go . . . somewhere?

— Why?

— Because I feel really uncomfortable about having you here.

— Why? I'm just a kid.

— Well . . . it just is really strange.

— What could be strange about our relationship, William?

— The video?

— Ah. What did you think of it?

— I thought it was a strange thing to send me.

— I got an 'A' for it in my 'media expression' prac at school.

— You're kidding.

— Yes. Yes, I am kidding. I died when I realised you could see down my top.

— Jane, you have to realise that yes at the moment you are changing from a little girl to a young woman and some men . . .

— Don't go all pervy, William. You're my big sister's boyfriend . . . You were my big sister's boyfriend. I think

175

it's a shame that just because you and her aren't really on, that you and I need to fall out of touch. I like you . . . liked you. You're like my uncle or something.

— But it's the uncles who are usually the weird ones.

— That's not the real uncles. That's just the 'Old Friend of the Family' uncles. They're the perverts.

— Well technically I am a 'Friend of the Family' uncle. She is Beautiful.

— Well don't get any ideas, Dopey. I just didn't want to go to school today.

— Jane, I am not getting ideas.

— Good. 'Cause I want to look through your stuff.

She sits up quickly and crawls, predates on all fours down to and off the end of my bed and looks through the contents of my large and fat wardrobe. On the right there are some shelves, three, the interior is dark and shadowy, and on the left is the 'hanging space'.

— Well at least your clothes are neat.

— My mother does my washing.

— That is so pathetic.

— I know it's pathetic. I try to stop her.

— Try try try. You don't really 'Do' do you, William?

— I suppose not. Do you want this coffee?

— Do you have any of Margaret's stuff here?

— No.

— You must. Where would . . . up here hidden behind the jumpers.

She half turns and says to me over her shoulder:

— You would hide them behind your jumpers. We don't want to really flaunt the fact that Margaret stayed over in front of your mother. Ah ha.

She returns to the shelves and pulls out a burgundy, satin shirt that Margaret has left here.

— I love this shirt. I really love this shirt. I was wondering what she'd done with it.

She turns and looks at herself in the mirror on the back of the left wardrobe door. Holds the shirt up in front of her, and runs her hands slowly down, slowly, particularly slowly, as her hands ride down and over her breasts. I stand, against the wall, holding the coffees, watching her reflection.

— Can I steal this?

— I suppose so. I thought you were too grown-up for stealing.

— True, she says and tosses the shirt onto my bed. I only steal microfilm. Nazi microfilm.

She returns her attention to my hidden stash of Margaret's belongings:

— The dumb, red scarf . . . we can throw that away. A couple of hair-clips . . . a scrunchie . . .

She brings out the bra. Margaret's and my black bra that I found on the floor. There is some carpet fluff on the cups which she picks off, and she turns to her reflection and holds the bra up against her. She forces her small breasts up into a slight cleavage. I can hear her breathing, a slight, small 'hmmm'. She looks at her face, I can see her staring into her eyes, considering, and then she winces, frowns, moderately creases her brow, and then, suddenly, as if she has made her mind up about something she reaches down, crosses her arms and takes the hem of her jumper.

— Jane, stop.

— No, she says, pulling her jumper up and over her head.

— Jane, really stop this. This is really nerdy.

— No, she says and drops the jumper onto the floor, still clutching her sister's crumpled up black bra in one hand.

— Well, if you want to try on your sister's underwear I think I'll go and sit in the other room.

— Stay there.

— Jane, I'm out of here.

— Just . . . chill, William.

— Okay. Okay. Fuck it. I'll stay. But when this story is retold and when I'm the jerk in the story or you crack the punchline, just know that I'm not really taken in by this, whatever it is.

— Sure, whatever Billy-boy, she says dismissively, as she watches her reflection, corrects her slightly mussed hair, undoes the buttons on the cuffs of the sleeves of her school shirt, and then puts her arms up the back of her shirt and does that amazing thing where a girl fumbles and bumbles around in her shirt for a few moments and then magically a bra appears. In this case it is a small white one, with—at the meeting of the two cups—a pale blue flower with a plastic pearl in its centre.

She drops it to the floor.

— Actually Jane, this is really getting a bit weird. I'm . . . I am just going to bail out . . .

— Just . . . William, just . . . bear with me . . . it's just . . . yeah it's a bit weird and I'm a bit freaked too but it's . . . I'm doing a thing, William. A sort of 'me' thing that I really have to do.

— Jane . . .

— No, please. Please don't keep on blathering. Just . . . shut the fuck up actually and just stand right where you are. I've gone over this scene a hundred times in my head and the way it works is that you shut the fuck up and stay still.

The black bra disappears up under her shirt.

— I really have worked out how this all happens. You'll just have to trust me.

— Well Jane, do I really have to be here?

— No. No, actually. You can go now.

— Okay.

— What? Were you really going to go then, William?

— Yes.

— Well please stay. Do stay. This'll only take a minute . . . at least that's how I've kind of worked it out.

And I have worked it all out. Well most of it.

I didn't know there'd be a rhino photo.

That was a surprise.

But we worked that through.

Her hands reappear, without the black bra.

— I didn't know you'd be clean-shaven. Sometimes I pictured you with a five-o'clock shadow, sometimes shaven. I'm pleased you are. I didn't know you'd have a mirror on the back of your cupboard door. I'm glad it's here.

She leans forward and stares into her eyes, runs one hand's fingers down from the base of her nose, slowly down and over her lips, making them fubble-fubble fubble as her fingers let them go. She looks into the mirror, looking over her reflected shoulder, and looks at me in the glass.

— I knew you'd look pretty weirded-out. That's cute.

— Jane . . .

— Don't talk. You really don't talk. I don't think you've got another line actually.

She starts unbuttoning her school shirt, starts with the top button and then the next.

— I didn't know this other shirt would be here but that's good.

Her shirt is undone, the front hangs open, and the black bra hangs haplessly about an inch under her small, firm breasts.

— I knew my sister's bra would be too big for me. By the way, I had planned on it being here. Did you know that was my idea? I told Margaret to leave one here; to mark you, to mark her territory. To spray you.

She drops her school shirt off her shoulders and again cups and lifts her breasts together. She puts her hands on her sides, and turns slightly, frowning, and regarding her figure.

She puts on the other shirt, the burgundy satin shirt. She doesn't button it.

— Sometimes I just turned up. I didn't say a word and you didn't say a word and we just, sort of . . . thing.

Dull hey?

Stop. Don't talk, William.

Don't answer.

For a while it was like . . . remember that time you drew the tattoo on my shoulder? You know when I was going to that party and I was meant to look like a punk and I got you to draw a tattoo on my shoulder. Of course you do. I couldn't breathe. Did you see that I just couldn't breathe? I saw that you couldn't breathe. Wasn't that such a . . . hell, I don't know . . . thing-moment. Just you and I. It was so kind of sexy. I imagined what it would be like to have you kind of have sex with me . . . my big sister's boyfriend having sex with me of all people.

Like . . . the kid sister.

Like . . . here's this big Uni type guy and he and Margaret are always out and he lives in this cool house and I just don't know about any of the things he talks about and haven't been to the places he's been or read the books or anything . . . and yet he still likes me. He still sees something in me. Even though I'm like nothing, like this little brat he still . . . sees me behind Margaret. Sees that I'm there too.

You fucked me because I've got a fucked older sister and she's a fucking pain and I hate living in her fucking shadow. I hate her setting my life for me. I hate being outdone by her. I hate discovering new things that she already knows. I want to find things for myself, not because she shows me.

Now . . . more recently, more recently when I've worked this thing through, it's happened just like this.

I start undoing the buttons on my skirt . . . two buttons see . . . and let it fall to the floor and kick it to the corner. My shoes and socks are off.

You didn't notice that.

I did that before. While you were in the kitchen. I figured the 'taking the shoes off' thing would be difficult; struggling around with my socks and undoing the laces and all. It troubled me. So I took them off while you were making the coffee.

That's bullshit actually. See . . . Margaret once told me that taking off shoes can always be the most awkward and 'unco' moment. She told me. I'll never find out for myself.

I'm cross that I will never ever in my life find that out for myself.

That was mine to discover.

That was mine to learn.

But no, Bitch-face took it away from me.

'It was really weird because then I had to take my shoes off and it took so long and he lost his hard-on and . . .'

Fuck Up, Fuck Up, Fuck Up and Fuck Off.

I want to find life by myself.

Anyway . . . I think I did alright.

I think I've worked it all out well. I knew this would work out because . . .

I'm kind of beautiful.

That was a critical factor.

I had to be beautiful.

And I am.

That's not vain, is it?

I think I'm fairly cute. I'm fairly cute.

This wouldn't be happening for a lesser girl.

For the dumpy and pimply, shy and ungainly little sister.

If I were her, you and I wouldn't have even thought this up.

And we've both worked this out, William. We've both planned and imagined and willed this into being.

I've worked it all out down to the finest detail.

Now I take these off.

'These' notice.

Not undies, or knickers, or panties. But . . . 'these'.

I could never work out what I would call them when I was here with you.

There's no nice word for a woman's underpants.

Finally, I settled for 'these'.

Wouldn't panties have jarred?

If I had have said 'Now I take my panties off', wouldn't it have clunked into the moment?

She pushes up her shirt with her wrists and runs her hands over her backside, her perfect backside, her glorious backside, her sweet arse. Then lifts her hands up and under the elastic and cups her hands on the cheeks of her arse.

— Now I lift them away from my . . . bum? Buns? Arse . . . and let them fall down my legs. Down my legs and I kick them off and away with my foot.

I clench my arse cheeks see?

Jane looks at her reflection, tries to cover her thick pubic hair with the corners of her shirt and stops.

— I am so fucking nervous here. I didn't know I'd be this nervous. Well I did but I didn't. I have to turn around now and come to you. Oh fuck fuck fuck fuck fuck fuck shit. Fuck . . . this is too weird. I'd planned to turn to you but I don't think I can.

Yes I can.

Not a chance.

Yes I can.

I can.

No way.

Jane turns around and faces me.

She is so beautiful.

We have never seen a woman like this. Her eyes are full, tears brimming to spill. And a sweet, slight smile with a kiss perfectly conspicuous in the right-hand corner, that maybe no one would ever claim.

— I kind of um . . . William it's about time for me as a . . . like in terms of where I am as a female and all I'd . . . like to . . . and now that we're like friends and all, not just . . . Margaret's little bitch-sister and . . . I'd like to . . . thing. With you, I mean, Jane says and takes one step forward, catches her foot under the bottom of the open wardrobe door, slips on a piece of newspaper, and falls with a thump on her bum.

— Well I didn't plan on that, she says and then bursts into tears.

I stand there.

— Don't just stand there, you shit. Don't just leave me here alone.

Then, on a Tuesday afternoon, Tuesday the 17th of some month, I went over to my ex-girlfriend's fifteen-year-old little sister, took her under the arm and lifted her up and onto my bed.

I knelt before her and held her sore foot to my mouth and kissed the slight wood burn that had appeared.

I knelt up, and we looked at each other's faces, she touched the red spot on the side of my nose, and I kissed the underside of her hand and then kissed her on the mouth.

She lay back on my bed and I lay beside her and undressed, kissed her cheek, her neck, her breasts and her belly and then cupped her vagina in my hand, and then gently entered and roused into her with my fingers.

She pushed me onto my back and lifted herself over and onto my penis, slowly eased me into her, an involuntary start, and then she stared at me, rested her hands on my stomach, and we found our rhythm, and slowly and quietly made perfect love.

Four times.

No we didn't.

I'm lying.

I didn't do that.

We didn't do that.

— I kind of um . . . William it's about time for me as a
. . . like in terms of where I am as a female and all I'd . . .
like to . . . and now that we're like friends and all, not just
. . . Margaret's little bitch-sister and . . . I'd like to . . .
thing. With you, I mean, Jane says and takes one step
forward, catches her foot under the bottom of the open
wardrobe door, slips on a piece of newspaper, and falls
with a thump on her bum.

— Well I didn't plan on that, she says and then bursts
into tears.

I stand there.

— Don't just stand there, you shit. Don't just leave me
here alone.

— I'm sorry.

— What do you mean you're sorry?

— I can't make lov . . . do this, Jane.

— What?

— I can't . . . I can't do this again.

— Can't fucking do what again?

— Here, I say and pass her her coffee, in what I think
must be one of the most unusual and incorrect actions ever
taken at any time ever in history.

— Ta, she says and puts the coffee down beside her.

— Do what again?

— What?

— Can't do what again?

— Oh. I can't . . . since I've been having sex I've done
just about every shitty, crappy, sleazy sex thing you can
do with the exception of four that I'm damn eager to try

185

but I can't . . . it has to stop. I'm sorry. You're very beau-
tiful, Jane. In a perfect world . . . I really do like you, Jane.
Pause.
— Get fucked, William.
— I'm sorry.
— No, get fucked. This isn't about your shit. It's not
about working out your mental shit. It's about working
out my shit.
— I can't.
— You shit. You fucking dumb shit.
— I'm sorry, I say and lean across to hold her.
— Don't touch me.
She grabs her jumper and pulls it on.
— Don't ever touch me. Don't ever talk to me. Do you
know what I just did? Just die. Don't die. Don't live. Just
don't ever be around me again.
— I'm sorry.
— Don't talk. Don't talk you fucking, ugly, fat, juvenile
shit. As if I would even think about sleeping with someone
like you. You really got me the wrong way, stupid. As if
I'd even think about it.
This was . . . this was just a complete stir.
She is haphazardly dressed now. I pass her one of her
shoes and she squeezes and stuffs her foot into it. I pass
her the other shoe and she hits me across the face with
the heel.
— None of this happened. None of this happened. I'm
out of here. I'm going to school.
She grabs her bag.
— I never want to see you again. I mean it.
You are never ringing our house again.
Ever.
She leaves.

She marches up to the front door and fumbles with the handle. Has to drop her bag to open the deadlock while maintaining pressure on the door handle.

Can't.

— Fucking open this fucking door.

I open the door and let her out and the door closes behind her, dragging on the carpet, and then is shut.

Fuck.

I flick the kettle back on, go and stand in the bedroom. Her bra is lying in the corner, she must still be wearing her sister's. And I think she's actually got on one of my socks because there's one of hers.

I walk into my lounge room, straighten the tassels on my rug with my toes, and then lean on the table and pick up a beer bottle top that's sitting like a small bowl.

I turn it over, and then around in my fingers so I'm looking at it straight on. There's a deer on it. Or a moose. No, it's a deer.

It's got a deer on it.

The doorbell rings.

I look up through the glass set in the door and can see the same silhouette that was there about a quarter of an hour ago. It presses itself up against the glass and becomes comparatively clear and discernible and Jane silently mouths the words:

— Let me in.

I open the door and stand aside as Jane enters past me, pushes past me, and drops her school bag in the middle of my lounge room.

She slaps me across the face.

Then slaps me again, and with both hands, and then grabs my cheeks and digs, digs her fingernails in.

Ouch.

I grab, hold her wrists, and we stand there. She stops trying to dig my cheeks from my face and just holds, rests her hands against the side of my face. She is furious. And she is crying. She hates me. I love her. She hates me and I love her. I lean forward and kiss her, pull her body towards and against me and then lift her up and carry her into my bedroom and there we make love. Folds her body onto me, lifts herself over and takes me into her, sets her palms on my chest and eases herself slowly up and down on me, measure by measure letting more and more of me in, and smiles and winces and grins through the pain . . .

Margaret

The final fucking word goes to me.

I have moved in with John and we enjoy a blissful peace and stability, sitting in front of open fires drinking fine red wines, and dipping crisp crackers in fresh dips and pâtés and cheese roulade. We sit with his fine-clad friends, and late at night over dying candles and with the hum of dishwashers and Van Morrison murmuring in the background, we talk about mortgages and the opera, skiing and sexual politics, theatre and sales. This friend here is one with whom John went to school, and now you may see him any day going to an office, carrying a little bag and an umbrella. This one married a lady of title and so became a lord. And another is a judge in a wig coming out an iron door. We are giants dressed in giants' robes. A charming clique and any stray faerie or hobo or derelict or lost child pressing their faces against the window and staring in and watching us embrace each other in our circle of warmth would think us the most splendid people in all the world. And John's house is wonderful, so perfectly decorated and fitted on the advice of magazines. I have my own study and my own mountain bike and all. It is a charmed existence. I am home.

Of an evening when John comes in from the hunt he throws the greatest fucking big chickens and turkeys on the table, pre-plucked and pre-herbed and pre-seasoned, they tell boring stories—I guess you can't paint a chook and call it a peacock, but they're fucking tasty.

After dinner we sit on the couch before the fire, I rest my head on his strong chest, his manly providing chest, clad in his Lacoste shirt, and sometimes when it's all very quiet, I can hear his heartbeat from behind the cloth and within the little crocodile emblem ticking as steadily as a clock.

I'm fucking happy here. Oh so fucking happy. This is where I always wanted to fucking be in my life. This is a happy fucking place. So fuck what you're thinking. I fucking deserve this. Fuck what you're thinking because I like living in a fucking nice place with a fucking rich partner and my mountain bike has twenty-one gears. Twenty-one. Count 'em.

I occasionally see William, though I do hear of him through Jane. They have not yet gone public about their relationship, quite correctly, but I know when she goes off to see him, and when she tells our parents that she's sleeping around at Wendy's house.

I don't begrudge Jane the experience. She'll have fun. But she'll move on eventually and then I suppose William will hook up with some other young missy, who will be his mother in turn, and thus it will go on, so long as men are gay and innocent and heartless.

Oh, there was something else . . . I figure it's probably important to the telling of how this whole thing panned out.

See . . . Jane's pregnant.

That's about it, I guess.

The William and me story.

NO SAFE PLACE
Mary-Rose MacColl

Shortlisted for the *Australian*/Vogel Literary
Award

Adele Lanois is Registrar of Walters
University and chief investigator in a sexual
misconduct case. A lone woman in a
powerful institution, Adele is unsure of
herself, unsure of her colleagues and
increasingly unsure that anything in her life
is quite as it seems.

A novel about sex, power and personal
responsibility, *No safe place* is a
contemporary thriller with the unexpected at
every turn.

1 86448 174 9

LISTENING FOR SMALL SOUNDS
Penelope Trevor

Shortlisted for the *Australian*/Vogel Literary
Award

Listening for small sounds is the story of
Joss, a young girl trapped in the tensions of
her parents' tangled marriage. Her days are
full but her nights are long as she lies in her
bed and listens for small sounds to determine
the mood of her unpredictable and violent
father. Often funny, sometimes unbearably
sad, Joss' story is one of strength,
acceptance, and above all, family.

1 86448 145 5